Layla Deen
and the Popularity Contest

Yahiya Emerick

ISBN: 1450527396
EAN-13: 9781450527392

**In the Name of Allah,
The Compassionate, the Source of All Mercy**

1

What should have been over in forty-five minutes seemed to have taken at least as many days, or so Layla thought, half-heartedly trying to cheer herself up. Shifting in her hard plastic seat to get even *more comfortable* for the umpteenth time, she tried hard not to doodle any further in her notebook, covered as it was now in a dizzying array of smiley faces, odd geometric shapes, flowers and different takes on forming the letters that made up her name.

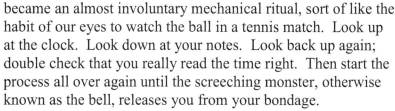

She looked up at the clock hopefully. The last five minutes. They were the worst, for it was within them that the habit of checking the time became an almost involuntary mechanical ritual, sort of like the habit of our eyes to watch the ball in a tennis match. Look up at the clock. Look down at your notes. Look back up again; double check that you really read the time right. Then start the process all over again until the screeching monster, otherwise known as the bell, releases you from your bondage.

The droning sound of Mr. Brown's voice had faded a long time ago into something remarkably similar to the sound of giant hermit crabs munching on food sticks. It wasn't that she didn't like school, (as far as any teenager could like school). She liked to learn new things and to be challenged.

But Mr. Brown was one of *those* teachers. You know the type: they just love to hear the sound of their own voices-*endlessly*. Teaching for them is a long process of lecturing students to death in order to enlighten them. (Mr. Brown also thought that it's a great way to catch students *sleeping* so he can punish and scold them for not paying attention!)

An abrupt change in Mr. Brown's tone drew Layla out of her temporary musings on what she would do differently if *she* were a teacher.

"Any questions?" he asked. (Long pause as the teacher scans a pathetic lot of bored faces.) "All right then. Read chapter 11 for homework, and then do the questions at the end. *All* of them."

Just then the bell sprang to life, causing more than one student to jolt involuntarily from the unexpected shock. Where there were half-asleep students before, now there was suddenly a stampede of wild teenagers all rushing for the door. Layla took her time. She knew all she had to look forward to was second period and yet *another* class that wasn't all that enjoyable. She stacked her thick literature book on her blue denim notebook, paused to throw the end of her headscarf over her shoulder, and then shoved the items in her navy blue backpack.

Joining the throngs in the halls of this school meant a crash course in stunt driving. Like great rushing rivers of flesh, an incomprehensibly tight flow of students wove their way through the halls in a deafening swell of noise and clamor. One lane rushed in one direction, another followed the opposite route. To accidentally stray into the gravity of the wrong flow was to risk getting swept away for a good solid two or three minutes.

Occasionally, a thick knot of students would form at an odd corner or door momentarily interrupting the flow, and it was through the skillful exploitation of gaps in the lines of the crowd that enabled Layla to get from point *A* to point *B* quickly, at least on most days. Today was one of her lucky days and she sidled up to her locker in record time.

"*Hey, Layla!*" cried a loud voice from behind her. "You can't avoid me *forever.*" Layla, who was just beginning to rummage through her locker, rolled her eyes privately and braced herself for the inevitable. A heartbeat later a sandy brown-haired girl wearing jeans and a bright yellow sweater stepped out from behind a mob of students, all rushing through the hall to get to their next classes on time.

"So whada'ya think?" She asked excitedly as she ambled up next to her intended captive audience. "Should I enter the contest *or not?*"

Layla put the last of her schoolbooks in her locker and slammed it shut with a bang. A quick glance sideways at the impatient face of her friend told her that she wouldn't be able to melt away into the crowds of passing students without giving an answer first. God knows she's 'disappeared' enough times over the last two days already to be able to get away with it again.

Layla turned her brown eyes up in exasperation, adjusted her black headscarf absent-mindedly, and replied in an uncertain tone of voice, "I *guess* so, Michelle. But why do you care about some *popularity* contest anyway? I mean, do any of those things really *mean* anything in the grand scheme of things?"

Layla paused and thought about the vapid *Popularity Contest* that she had heard about. After glancing at all the faces in the throngs passing by, she continued her line of reasoning, saying, "Either people like you or they don't and I don't see how winning or losing in a *vote* would change that."

"I don't think *you* know what this is all about," Michelle chided playfully. "If you're not that popular right now, just being *in the contest- and having everyone know it-* will make you even *more* popular than you were before. Then I can move up from there on the social ladder and who knows? Maybe I'll win – or maybe next year - and then I'll show those snotty girls up. *That* would be *sooo* cool."

"Look," Layla responded, as she pulled her friend aside to avoid being swept away by a big bulge of students rushing a bit too close, "I've got to get to gym class on time or the teacher will make me do a *million* push ups or something. He's got it in for me, you know. We'll talk about this later. Give me a call or something."

"Okay," Michelle nodded, as she bobbed her head, almost pleadingly. "I'll call you at about seven or, *oh-* wait a minute. My *shows* are on tonight. I'll call you after nine-thirty or so. Okay?"

"That's fine." Layla responded curtly. "I gotta' go *right now*." She waved with her one free hand while shouldering her backpack with the other and then took off down the hall racing towards the gymnasium. Michelle waved once herself and then realized she was going to be late for her next class, as well. She darted down the beige colored hall in the opposite direction, pondering over what her new found popularity might mean.

Layla looked at the big round clock on the wall just above the stairs leading down to the first floor of the school building. Its white face and large block type numbers seemed to leer back at her, as if to say, "*You're late - again.*" She also noticed that the crowds in the hallway were thinning out considerably. It looked like most of the students had reached their classes already, leaving only a few stragglers scampering by here and there.

She knew she would really have to get a move on if she wanted to avoid the wrath of Mr. Rathburn. He was the only teacher she was truly afraid of, not because he might fail her on the report card, but because he often made her do all sorts of awful calisthenics as punishment for even the smallest infractions, *and he always seemed to find something to punish her for.*

Realizing she might not make it on time, she sprinted into a steady jog. Up the steps and through the long hall she went. She could see her target – the doors to the gym - just up ahead. She slowed down slightly to catch her breath (no need to *look* like you were running to class when you come in).

She was just about to open the door to the gymnasium when suddenly a loud alarm rang out through the halls. The bluntness of the late bell nearly caused her heart to jump out of her body, after all, the only thing she had been focusing on in her mind's eye was Mr. Rathburn's scowling face, and the bell seemed to be his barking voice.

It's not like he was an *evil* teacher or anything, mused Layla, as she turned the door handle to the gym. He was hard on everybody. But he didn't even try to hide his special resentment for Layla Deen.

When she had first entered Junior High almost two years earlier, her mother had made a request to the school that Layla be allowed to wear a jogging suit and her *hijab*, or head covering, during gym classes. The dress code for female students in the gym at that time was shorts and a short sleeve shirt with no hats allowed.

Layla, being an observant Muslim girl, just didn't want to wear so *few* clothes. She didn't want to feel so *exposed*. Islam, her way of life, had very clear guidelines on how a respectable girl should dress in public: loose clothes, long sleeves, pants and a head covering to hide her hair so boys wouldn't be able to judge her by her looks alone.

Mr. Rathburn refused her mother's request at first saying every one of the girls had to wear shorts and a T-shirt. Well, it became a big stink with the office and Layla's mother threatened to sue the school. Mr. Rathburn was forced to back down and even though Layla was a good gym student and participated fully, he never seemed to forget his grudge against her. Some of the more athletic girls in gym, who were total teachers' pets, also seemed to be hostile towards her at times - probably to gain favor with Rathburn. This made gym class one of Layla's most trying periods of the day.

Layla had just slipped through the gym door and was hoping to slip into the girls' locker room unnoticed, but it just wasn't meant to be.

"What's *this*!" A coarse male voice barked out, startling Layla out of her momentary recollection. "*Deen*? *Late again*!"

Some of the other girls, who were just filing out of the locker room and lining up on the hardwood gym floor, giggled and laughed at the fate that had befallen the unpopular late-comer. Linda Patterson, one of the most outgoing girls in the school, smirked, "Loser!" She arched her neck and pointed, causing the other girls gathered around her to snicker. Layla just ignored the taunting and stopped dead in her tracks.

She turned to face the dreaded gym teacher who was coming over in her direction, all the while fearing the worst. Although Layla was rarely late to gym, she knew it would be pointless to argue with Mr. Rathburn. He was constantly looking for ways to punish the girl who had dared to oppose his will.

"I should give you detention for being so late!" He growled. Then he put both fists on his waist and tried to suck in his overwhelming *girth* to look even more hard nosed.

Layla wasn't more than a few seconds late and they both knew it, but the ritual had started and they both knew where it was headed.

"After you get dressed in your *garbage bag* suit I want you to run twenty laps around the whole gym before you can join the class!" He said menacingly.

Layla nodded her head dejectedly and headed towards the locker room. The girls standing in the line at the edge of the yellow hardwood court hooted and smirked. Layla glanced downwards as she continued towards the entrance and steeled herself against the unfavorable looks she was receiving - and would continue to receive - all throughout the class.

Once safely inside the now deserted locker room, Layla could hear the shouts of the girls as they began to play floor hockey outside in the gym. The heated calls and cries of the game echoing faintly through the walls made for an eerie experience in this otherwise empty, cold, gray-tiled chamber. Trying to pull some more hope out of her nearly empty reservoir of strength, she dropped her bag by her locker and sat down on the bench to take a deep breath.

Layla's futile exercise in centering herself was quickly interrupted by the realization that Rathburn would be timing her, even in here, so she swiftly changed into her sweat suit and gym shoes and then adjusted her *hijab* so it would fit more tightly. She was just about to leave the locker room to start her laps when she was suddenly startled by a sharp "*ping*" on the floor from somewhere in the adjacent shower area.

She listened for a moment and then called out, "Who's there?" Hearing nothing she added, "If you're late Mr. Rathburn will make you run twenty laps like me."

Layla waited for a reply but none came. She thought she heard some kind of muffled muttering.

"C'mon," she called out again, "who's there?" Hearing nothing further she put her foot on a nearby bench, adjusted the laces on her shoes one more time and then slowly crept along the row of tall, pewter colored lockers until she reached the entrance to the group shower area.

Layla never showered there after gym class. The idea of everyone showering all *together* repulsed her. She could never do that and it was one of the more unpleasant aspects of public school life for her.

"Hello?" Layla inquired, though a bit louder this time. "Anyone there?"

Another loud "ping" echoed sharply off the walls of the shower room followed by a low voice cursing, "Darn it!"

Layla peered around the corner of the dimly lit shower area. It smelled musty and humid, as always. As her eyes adjusted to the low light she saw the figure of a girl bent down in the far corner, trying to pick something up hurriedly off the moist, brown checker-tiled floor. The girl's back was turned to her, but Layla knew almost instantly who it was. Her jet-black hair, ripped leather jacket and tight black leggings with the chunky combat boots; it could be no one other than Kelly Spitz.

"Whada' you want?" Kelly growled menacingly as she turned her head slightly in Layla's direction. "Aren't you supposed to be in gym or something with all the other *prissies*?"

Layla noticed Kelly shoving some things in her purse and then answered, "I came late and Mr. Rathburn's making me run laps. I heard a noise and I just..."

But before Layla could finish, Kelly stood up and without making eye contact rushed past her, clutching her black purse tightly.

"*Whatever*." She huffed, as she ran for the emergency exit in the rear of the locker room. In an instant she bolted out the door and onto the grassy soccer field behind the gym. The door slowly swung shut behind her and sealed itself with a small click. Layla barely had time to think about what had just happened when a loud booming voice suddenly sent shivers through her spine. "*Deen*! What happened? You get *lost* in there or something? Get out here now!"

Layla realized that Mr. Rathburn, who was standing just inside the door of the girls' locker room, would probably come in looking for her if she waited another moment. "Coming!" she yelled, as she turned towards the door.

As Layla slid by him and out into the brightly lit gymnasium, Mr. Rathburn snarled, "For being late *again* you got ten more laps added. Now do thirty!"

Layla was about to protest but the look on his face told her he would go even higher in the number of laps if she said anything. Silently, she began her run around the circumference of the large gymnasium, all the while noticing how much fun the other girls were having with their long plastic hockey sticks as they played, cheered and shouted.

By the time she finished all her laps, gym was half way over. She had made sure to jog slowly so as not to become too tired but it was still quite a punishment this time, especially because her sweat suit was made of nylon, not cotton.

She stopped to take her last breath and then headed over to the sidelines where her tormentor stood. Mr. Rathburn, seeing her approach, scowled and gave her a floor hockey stick and told her to play defense on the losing team.

She did very well, blocking two goals, but no one said anything to her. She didn't have any friends in this class. Except for the fact that she liked sports, this was her least favorite period. "Oh well," she thought morbidly, "it'll *all* be over one day soon."

She found herself wondering, however, whenever the puck was on the other side of the court, about Kelly Spitz and what she had been doing alone in the locker room. The rigors of the floor hockey game kept distracting her, though, and she soon forgot about the incident.

2

"*Assalamu 'alaykum*, Mom," Layla announced as she opened the front door to her house. [1]

A muffled reply came from the kitchen, "*Wa 'alaykum assalam*, dear."

Layla dropped her book bag inside the door and wondered why it always seemed like she brought a whole locker's worth of books home everyday whether she did most of her homework in school or not.

"How was school, today?" Layla's mother asked as she walked out of the kitchen with a mixing bowl in her hand.

"Oh," Layla sighed, noticing the sunlight coming in from the window behind her mother, "It was okay."

"Just *okay*?"

"Well, you know, school is, *well*, school."

Layla's mother hugged her daughter with her one free hand and replied, "I know, I didn't like school very much either when I was your age. Do you have any homework?"

Layla pointed silently to her bulging back pack and Layla's mother nodded gravely in understanding.

"Then I'll have Hafsa help me with dinner tonight."

---

[1] This is the Muslim greeting of, "Peace be upon you."

"Okay." Layla responded as she kicked off her black, chunky-heeled shoes and then willed herself to pick up her now enormous-seeming book bag again and haul it upstairs to her room.

She climbed the stairs wearily and opened the door to her bedroom. "Ah, *sanctuary*," she thought to herself, as she threw the bag down by her desk and flopped back-first onto her bed. She lay there for a few minutes, savoring the softness of the mattress, staring at the ceiling and thinking about nothing in particular.

After a while she sat upright, took off her *hijab* and went to the upstairs bathroom to do her *wudu*, or ritual washing, so she could offer her late afternoon prayer. Islam taught that prayer, five times a day, was a religious duty and Layla was very conscientious about her duties.

Returning to her room, she laid out her red prayer rug facing in the direction of Mecca, tied a special scarf she wore for this purpose around her hair and stood silently in the contemplation of the black clothed building called the Ka'bah in faraway Mecca. That was the House of God. Not a place where God *lived*, but a special shrine in the shape of a simple cube, two stories high, whose purpose was to unite all people into one orientation of Godliness.

Layla began her prayer with a silent intention to offer her praise to God and then raised her hands slowly up to just below her shoulders. Pausing momentarily, she softly uttered the first words of the daily ritual, "*Allahu akbar*," or "God is greater," the unfinished sentence implying that God is greater than *anything*.

For the next several minutes she recited some verses from the Qur'an, bowed and then prostrated in a series of four such choreographed movements. When she finished her *salat*, she sat quietly in the stillness of her room and recited a few lines of praise for God called *dhikr*. Then she cupped her hands in front of her and asked God in her own words for strength, guidance and forgiveness.

Feeling a bit refreshed, as her prayers always made her feel, Layla folded up her rug and laid it on the bottom shelf of her nightstand. Then she stood in front of her bureau mirror and proceeded to comb her long shiny black hair out. A few minutes later she changed into some loose beige pants and a light yellow long-sleeved T-shirt.

Ahmad, her older brother, was still at school. He was on the track team in High School and often stayed after school to practice. Hafsa, her younger sister, would be home any time now. She was a third grader, though she acted sometimes as if she thought she were the boss of everybody.

Layla sighed again, savoring the brief moment of peace she was still blessed with. A few moments later she willed herself to reenergize and began to unpack her book bag. Then, after stacking up her books on her desk in the order of hardest

homework to easiest, she sat down in her chair and began to work.

Her system served her well: do the hardest tasks first while you still have the energy to do them. Then the easier work will follow in its own good time.

About half an hour later, Layla lifted her head up from her studies to listen. She had just heard the sound of the front door

slamming shut as the hurricane, otherwise known as *Hafsa*, blew in. Although she had closed her door before, Layla could still hear Hafsa running to hug her mother. Excited news about little kid things poured from her mouth in a daily ritual as old as when Hafsa could first speak. Then Layla braced herself for the inevitable pounding of tireless little feet coming up the stairs.

A few minutes later, Hafsa came running as expected and opened Layla's door with a swish. *Of course* the idea of *knocking* was completely foreign to her. "*Assalamu 'alaykum, Layla Dayla!*" The overly energized little girl shouted.

"*Wa 'alaykum assalam, Hafsa Bafsa!*" Layla called back, slightly annoyed. Hafsa's word games and weird name rhymes had been a constant feature of life for as long as she could remember, especially because they never seemed to end.

Hafsa then ran out of the room and pushed open Ahmad's door and yelled something equally odd. Layla smirked when she thought of the expression on Hafsa's face when she realized that Ahmad wasn't home yet.

"*Hey,*" Hafsa intoned, quite disappointedly. "Where's Ahmad? *Is he still at practice?*"

"Yes, he is." Layla answered, as she got up and walked to her door. "Now be quiet and help mom with dinner 'cause I got homework to do."

"*All right, already.*" Hafsa answered in her best impression of an unfairly chastened little saint. "You don't have to *rush* me." With that, Hafsa swished her black shoulder length hair expressively and bounded back down the stairs and off into the kitchen. Layla returned to her work with a sigh.

A little while later Ahmad arrived home, though he didn't immediately come upstairs. He almost never seemed to have any homework. Instead, he went out back and started shooting baskets in the hoop he had installed himself over the garden shed.

About a half an hour after that, Layla's father pulled up in the driveway. He usually arrived home from work at about 6:00 and would thereafter hang around the living room for most of the rest of the night. Sometimes he would go directly out again to the *Masjid,* or Prayer Hall, if there was a meeting or something.

Layla, who was still busy with her algebra, science and creative writing homework, soon lost track of time. She hadn't even noticed the gradual setting of the sun and darkening of the skies outside her bedroom window. Abruptly, she was awakened from the Land of Endless Ink when she heard her mother call to her from downstairs, "Layla. Time for dinner."

Layla took a deep breath and then put her pen aside. It was warm from having been in her hand for so long and she bemusedly wondered how long it would take to cool down.

Standing up, she took a look around her room and its eclectic mixture of toys from her youth and gadgets that reflected her new interests and then she opened her door and headed straight for the upstairs bathroom. A moment later she appeared in the dining room where the rest of her family had already begun to seat themselves.

"*Assalamu 'alaykum*, daddy," she said as she went to kiss her father on the cheek.

"*Wa 'alaykum assalam wa rahmatullahi wa barakatuhu*, Layla. How was school today?"

"Fine," she answered, as she took her place at the table on the right side near the large double paned window.

"Ahmad," his father asked, "can you say the *du'a* before we eat?"

"Sure, Dad." Ahmad replied. He cupped his hands in front of him with his palms facing upwards to show he was asking to receive God's blessing, and the rest of the family did likewise.

"Allahumma baraklana feemaa razaqtana
wa qeena adhabin naar. Bismillahir Rahmaanir Raheem."

"O Allah, bless us in what You have provided for us
and protect us from the punishment of Hell-fire.
In the Name of Allah, the Compassionate, the Merciful."

After Ahmad finished saying grace, he and everyone else gently passed their open palms over their face to signify that they were washing the blessings of God on their faces; like bathing in God's light.

With that said the family began to enjoy their dinner of roast chicken, saffron rice, yams, flat bread and salad and talked about the day's events. Layla didn't say much and ate slowly. She hadn't been very talkative for the last two years now, ever since she had entered junior high. Her parents learned not to press her to talk about her experiences in school, though they were always ready to listen if she had a problem.

Layla, however, didn't want to bother her parents with too much about her life because on a certain level she felt a little embarrassed to complain to them about her problems. After all, her father worked so hard at his job and her mother still seemed quite sad about her own troubles with her relatives. When she converted to Islam, just before she met her husband and married him, her parents vowed to disown her and that's just what they did for a time.

After many years they had softened their dissonance a little bit, but Layla knew her mother never fully recovered from the shock and pain that her own loved ones put her through. Because of that, Layla barely had a relationship with her maternal grandparents and only saw them once a year when her family would take the daylong drive to visit them out of courtesy.

Such meetings grated on everybody, as the grandparents were sometimes so cold to their own grandchildren, just because they followed a different religion. "What problem could I have," Layla often thought to herself, "that would top my mother's pain?"

After dinner was finished, Layla, who had been lost in her musings on her troubles in school, helped her mom carry the leftover food into the kitchen. The family later prayed the sunset prayer together and then Layla went back upstairs to finish the last of her homework. This was a routine that Layla knew well. It was the rhythm of her life.

3

A loud chirping sound startled Layla out of her homework induced trance. It was late and she was right in the middle of a math story problem, trying to imagine a situation in which she would ever need to find the median average of three bushels of apples, when the noise from the phone by her bed brought her rudely back down to earth. Her parents had gotten her her own private phone as an 'Eid gift last year and for that she was eternally grateful, except for the fact that it was like a magnet for Hafsa, who often came in and spent hours talking to her little friends - all the while disturbing Layla's peace.

"*Yes*." Layla asked when she picked up the phone. Although she was a Muslim and preferred to say *Salam,* or peace, when answering the phone, she had both Muslim and non-Muslim friends who would call. She didn't want to say 'Hello' to her Muslim friends and she didn't want to say the Muslim greeting to her non-Muslim friends, so she thought a simple "Yes" was a good compromise.

"Layla. It's Michelle." the voice on the other line announced, almost triumphantly.

"Oh, how are you doing?" Layla replied, more than a little relieved to get a break from her homework.

"I'm fine. My shows are over now, so I wanted to call you so we could talk about the Popularity Contest."

"What time is it?"

"Almost ten o'clock."

"Wow, I didn't realize it was so late." In the back of her mind she realized her mother would probably be calling her for the late night prayer soon.

After putting Hafsa to sleep, her father most likely took Ahmad to the *Masjid* for congregational prayer, so it would be just her mother and her. Layla used to go to the *Masjid* quite often as well but for a while now she had had so much homework to do, she often stayed home and prayed alone with her mother.

"Did you do your homework yet?" Layla asked casually.

"Yeah, I finished all of it while I was watching TV." Michelle chirped, exuding satisfaction with herself.

Layla knew now why she was always the one with the better grades.

"So what do you think?" asked Michelle curtly. "Do you think that by just *entering* the contest I could possibly move up enough in the social ranks to win?"

Ever since the school pep squad announced the "Most Popular Kid in School" contest, it seemed to Layla that everyone had lost their mind. There was a big bulletin board set up outside the Student Council office where people could enter their names. After three weeks, the top five names on the list would be put on special ballots and circulated to the different classrooms where students could vote. The winner would get the title of the most popular student in the yearbook and also would get to represent the school at different events and functions.

"Michelle, I glanced at the list after third period and I only saw three names there: Linda Patterson, Shelly MacPherson and Shamika Thompkins. They're so popular that you might not have much of a chance to win."

Layla almost bit her tongue when she realized the import of her last remark, for she had to choose her words carefully. She didn't want it to seem that she was against her friend's prospects, especially since Michelle was one of her *only* friends in the whole school.

"All those girls are stupid." Michelle said defensively. "They're only there because they told people to put their names there. Now this puts me in a bind. You can't nominate yourself so I need someone to add my name to the list, too. I'd be tempted to just write it in myself, but there's always a crowd of people around there. Someone might see me. Layla, I need you to do me big favor."

Layla held her breath and knew right away what was coming.

"I need you to add my name to the list."

Layla fell silent for a brief moment. She hated everything to do with meaningless popularity issues. She had been burned enough times by the "popular girls" - their insults, mean looks and air of sickening superiority - to want to have anything to do with any part of their world or vapid interests.

"Can you imagine," Layla asked Michelle in carefully chosen words, "if people saw me going and writing on that list? They would tease me and humiliate me. Oh no, I *can't* do that. Why don't you ask Marcy or Lisa?"

"Because they don't think I can win and I would feel embarrassed to ask them. Can you imagine what they would say to me? '*Why do you want to be popular?*' or '*Who died and made you queen?*'"

"If you're too embarrassed to ask *them*, what makes you think you won't be embarrassed by other kids if they see me write your name there?"

"Because no one will care if they see you write it. They won't even pay attention."

"Gee, *thanks*." Layla said in a lilting voice.

"No, I didn't mean it that way. You know, everyone knows you're all good and everything. You wear that scarf and you don't say bad words. People will think you're being nice to your friend and they would never think I asked you to do it."

Layla twirled a finger in her hair and thought for a moment. Michelle was a better-than-average looking girl with pretty hair, and she always dressed in style. Although she wasn't a jock or a rich girl, she had no open enemies. She once had expressed an interest in joining the cheerleaders and was usually invited to people's parties and such. Maybe she would have half a chance.

"But what if you don't win?" Layla asked. "What if people don't vote for you simply because I put your name there, thinking they would be going against someone I was friends with?

"Oh, don't worry about that. The publicity may even help me. You know, the sympathy vote. So you'll do it?"

Layla puzzled a moment over the 'sympathy' part, unsure if even Michelle knew what she was saying, but then she realized that she had unwittingly been backed into a corner.

She had no other choice - at least if she wanted to keep Michelle as a friend. Although she had other friends, they were mostly the girls she knew from Sunday school and they lived kind of far away. No, she needed friends in her neighborhood and especially in her school if she was going to survive.

"All right," she sighed in resignation. "I guess I'll do it."

"Good. I expect to see my name there tomorrow. Thanks, you're such a *good* friend. Okay, 'gotta go. Talk to ya' later *chica*. Bye."

Layla heard the click and finally realized how Michelle was able to keep her own semi-popular network going, even in the face of the huge webs spun by Linda Patterson, Shelly MacPherson and Shamika Thompkins. Michelle was a classic busybody.

Layla plopped herself back on her bed and thought for a moment. She pondered over why *she* had to be unpopular, why *she* had few friends at school and why *she* was chosen for what seemed to be a life of misery. Ahmad had it so easy, she mused, and Hafsa, too.

She pictured the scenario over in her mind. She would be walking down the hall, slowly approaching the *Sign Up* board outside the Student Council office. Everyone would watch as she, the least likely of all people, would scribble someone's name on the board. Then, as she walked away, everyone would rush over to the off-white poster board sign and see whose name she wrote.

"Michelle will probably lose her contest as a side-effect of so many people disliking me," thought Layla. "Michelle will blame me and I'll lose another friend." Layla rolled over on her bed and considered her predicament. It wasn't always this way. She had had a lot of friends when she was in elementary school.

It was only when she entered junior high and was put with so many other *unfamiliar* kids that the trouble started. Some of the snobby girls started making fun of her *hijab* and then in what seemed no time she developed the unfair reputation of being *different* and thus *undesirable*. Layla didn't even want to contemplate what the kids always say to her when there's "terrorist" incidents in the news and the reporters blame all Muslims everywhere without asking why the many must be blamed for the actions of the very few.

This, of course, was a big burden for her to bear. In elementary school everyone liked her. In junior high, almost no one liked her. Layla went from being an open and out-going girl to being withdrawn and quiet. A good day for her now was when she could go through the day without some girl or another saying something or looking at her weirdly. None of the boys ever bothered her, though. They all knew about her brother, Ahmad, who was a skilled martial artist.

Everyone had heard of how he had learned kung fu in China and had saved another student from kidnappers. So out of respect - or fear - of Ahmad, the boys kept their distance. Some of them also seemed to respect her on account of her good manners and mature demeanor. But whatever the reason the boys didn't harass her, her brother had no leverage, however, over the attitudes of the girls in junior high.

Anyway, she didn't want his help even if he could offer it. She didn't want to feel that he had to stick up for her all the time. That would be even more humiliating. So she just suffered in silence. Some nights she would cry herself to sleep, other nights she would dream of revenge on those girls who made her life miserable.

Layla, realizing the time, stopped thinking about Michelle and her problems and also about her own and went downstairs and prayed her night prayer alone. Her mother had finished long before and had already turned in for the night. Looking around in the darkened house, sensing the heaviness in the air amid the dim moonlight faintly cascading through the window, she unfolded her red embroidered prayer rug once again and stood at attention, offering her words of praise to the Almighty.

Her supplications were followed by a few moments of sincere pleading to God to help her make it through the next day. She then returned to her own room thoughtfully and climbed into bed. Pulling the covers over her face, thoughts of the next day's task haunted her as she tried her best to drift off to sleep.

4

The bell ending third period spooked Layla out of her meandering trance. She didn't often daydream in class but this was one of those times when she just couldn't concentrate on Mrs. Jenkins and her American history lectures. Luckily, she hadn't been called on to answer any questions today. As she stood up to gather her books she said an involuntary, "*Alhumdulillah*," to herself which at this moment meant, *"Thank God the teacher left me alone."*

Layla tried not to think about it but she knew that Michelle was passing by the Student Council office between every period to see if her name had been written there on the bulletin board yet. Layla thought about what Michelle must have said to herself each time she came away disappointed: *"That Layla! Some friend she is. Humph!"*

The day was wearing on and Layla knew that if she was going to do the job it had better be soon. With a swish of her hand to adjust her scarf she walked out into the crowded hallway and began her usual pattern of ducking in and out between the throngs of students.

She finally made it to her locker in the next aisle and was just about to open the combination lock when she saw a little sticky note hanging out from the metal slits in the upper part of the door. She looked at it suspiciously and then tugged at it. It came out quite easily. She looked at it and found a message scrawled on one side. It read simply, "Don't think I've forgotten about you. I have a 'surprise' for you!"

"What!" Layla said, almost too loudly. "Now I'm being reminded?" She knew that Michelle was impatient but she never left annoying little notes before. And what was this about a surprise? Maybe, thought Layla, Michelle bought her a little gift like a fuzzy pencil or something as a reward for her trouble. Michelle was known for such gaudy things.

She frowned and then crumpled the note up and threw it at the bottom of her now opened locker. After she stacked her books for the next couple of periods in her arm, she made up her mind and gathered the courage to head straight for the Student Council office.

There were still a couple of minutes left before the next class was to begin, so to quickly go there and write a name shouldn't cause her to be late. She hated to go near that place, however, because of what happened the year before. During her freshmen year she wanted to run for the Student Council but it was during one of those weird times when there were troubles in the Middle East. Some people with Muslim-sounding names - but not Muslim self-control - were seen on TV shouting, "*Death to America!*"

Well, Layla, being the only Muslim girl in school who wore *hijab*, bore the brunt of the prejudice whipped up by the media. Although there were a few other kids in the school from Muslim families, they laid low and never identified themselves as Muslims. They avoided the scarf-wearing Layla like the plague.

Remembering the humiliation she endured, she stopped in mid-stride and gritted her teeth for a split second as she recalled how some of the members of last year's Student Council made up all kinds of weird rules and regulations at the last minute to disqualify her from even having her name considered. It was so unfair but Layla knew she couldn't do anything about it. At the same time, she didn't want to get her parents involved either. That might make matters worse and cause the other kids to think that she couldn't defend herself or something.

"Oh well," Layla sighed to herself as she woke up from her reminiscing. "They're all a bunch of losers anyway."

Layla continued on her way through the intersecting halls until she finally reached the Student Council office and found a bunch of students standing around in front of the open door. It was sort of like the hangout for the popular kids and their clique. If you were on the Student Council you could often get out of class on the made-up excuse that you had work to do for the Student Affairs Committee or for the administration or the pep squad.

Layla tried her best to ignore the stares of the seven or eight kids who were there and made her way straight to the brightly decorated bulletin board. In the center was a white poster board with the title in big, colorful letters:

Who's the Most Popular Kid in School? Nominate your Choices Here.

Layla saw the straight lines in the center where names were supposed to be written. There were a few names scrawled there already - the same names she saw before when she happened to notice the board for the first time a week earlier.

Not wanting to prolong this longer than she had to, she stepped up to the board and opened the zipper on a side pocket of her book bag. She had just begun to take a pen when suddenly a voice from behind startled her.

"Hey, *Lula*." That was the nickname some of the meaner students called her. "Whatcha doin'? Writing *yourself* in on the popularity contest? *That's* the biggest joke of the century!"

Layla turned around, already knowing who it was. Linda Patterson stood there in all her snotty glory. Her long blond hair styled in waves; her red baggy sweater and faded tight jeans; her high-heeled black boots - and of course, her nose turned up in arrogance and her lips pursed in a condescending scowl.

"I'm not writing my own name here." Layla protested. "I'm writing the name of a girl I think is more deserving than you are to be here."

"*Oh, is that so?*" Linda smirked wryly, eyeing her friends cheekily. "And who might *that* be?"

"Michelle Whitman."

"Ha! Michelle *Witless* is more like it. She's so lame. She doesn't have a snowball's chance in summer to beat me."

"Well, we'll see about that. You never know what'll happen in the future."

"Oh, that's right- you're all religious and stuff." Linda laughed. "But *I know* what's gonna' happen. She's gonna' lose and I'm gonna' laugh at her. But even more importantly, everyone's gonna' laugh at you after they see what you did!"

"And what is that?" Layla asked, slightly puzzled, "There's nothing wrong with nominating someone."

"Oh, sure, there's nothing wrong with writing your little friend's name on the list, but when everyone sees that you wrote your *own name* on the list for the popularity contest they're gonna' have a field day with you."

"What do you mean, *my* name?" Layla protested, almost dropping her book bag to the gray tiled floor. "I didn't write my name and nobody nominated me."

"Oh yeah?" Linda raised her arm triumphantly, pointing her manicured finger towards the list. "Then what's *that*!"

Layla turned her head and looked at the list. Right there, to her shock and horror, was the name: *Layla Deen*, written in clear and bold letters in the fourth slot, right under Shamika Thompkins.

Layla felt a rush of embarrassment and revulsion and immediately fumbled for an eraser from her pocket and was about to start erasing her name when Linda pushed in front of her and stood with her body in front of the bulletin board.

"Oh, no you don't." She commanded. "No one's allowed to alter or remove the names on this list. If you didn't write your name then someone must have nominated you and that's final!"

Layla knew Linda wouldn't back down. She was on the Student Council and was a favorite of the council's teacher-sponsor, Mrs. Rhone.

Layla pushed her anger down in the rusty room of her heart where she stored her oft-wounded pride, right next to a big rubbish pile of frustration and worry, and sighed.

It must have been that big surprise Michelle's note mentioned. "Why would she do this to me?" Layla wondered. Though the sound of students hurrying by brought her back to reality.

"Okay, whatever," she huffed. "But I still have to write Michelle's name on this list."

"Be my guest." Linda intoned slyly as she moved aside. The girls near her guffawed slightly and whispered to each other, all the while smirking and staring condescendingly.

Layla wrote Michelle's name on the last slot of the list and hurried away as quickly as she could. She made it to her next class on time but soon found that she couldn't bring herself to concentrate on the teacher's lecture.

All she could think about was the embarrassment she would have to go through when everyone would see her name on the 'Most Popular' ballots. Boy would that cause a lot of gossip, and some students might taunt her as well. For most of this year she had been pretty much left alone, save for the minor annoyances caused by Linda and a few others.

But the biggest dilemma facing her now was the puzzling problem of Michelle's betrayal. After all, Michelle was supposed to be her friend. Didn't she realize that it would be a *bad* thing, and *not* a good thing, for Michelle to enter her in that contest? Didn't she know the hassles and stress it would cause and wasn't she aware that it was the last thing Layla wanted?

In between looking like she was paying attention to the teacher, who was droning on about some dry fact, Layla alternated frantically inside her heart and mind between feelings of raw anger and a sorrowful sense of betrayal. Why did she do it? Was it so people would get distracted and not think about who wrote her name on the list?

The issue of *Layla Deen* nominating Michelle wouldn't even come up because the kids would be too busy teasing *the outcast* for having her name also appear in a contest that everyone knew she couldn't win. Suddenly, Layla felt the room grow a little warmer, but then she realized it must have been her own nervous reaction getting the better of her.

By the end of class Layla resigned herself to the inevitable. She was just going to have to weather another crisis in her tortured junior high career. She also decided not to say anything to Michelle about it. What would that gain? If she confronted Michelle, who must have thought it was no big deal, then she would get mad at her and she would assuredly lose her as a friend.

For the first time Layla gained a greater appreciation for the phrase that her father once taught her to say to describe situations just like this: *Like being caught between a rock and a hard place.*

Layla let out an audible sigh of relief when the bell ending class time rang. Then she gathered her things together and went out in the hall hoping she was ready to face the rest of the day.

As it turned out, she wound up not seeing Michelle for the remainder of the school day, which wasn't at all unusual, for Michelle was an assistant in the library and sometimes spent a lot of time there. An exercise in irony, thought Layla. But for once, Layla didn't mind not seeing her. She knew that if she did she would just have to smile and pretend everything was all right. She didn't want to have to put on a false face to a friend, no matter how mad she was at her, especially since she was so pressured to put on a front for everyone else.

The bus ride home seemed a blur and Layla almost missed getting off at her bus stop. The walk home through the quiet little tree-lined streets seemed even shorter. "For once," Layla thought, "I'm actually looking forward to homework. Maybe it'll distract me enough to where I'll forget about this whole mess, at least for a while."

5

"*Hey, Girl*!" Came a high-pitched, roaring voice into the phone so loudly that Layla had to move the receiver away from her ear for second. "Thank you, thank you, thank you, thank you *sooo* much for entering my name in the contest. I ran there at lunchtime and saw my name right there - almost in lights! This is so cool! I'm gonna' be voted the most popular. I know it! I'm a library assistant, all the teachers like me, my grades are in *okay* shape and I'm friends with everyone! Not to mention I'm beautiful, too, but you didn't hear me *say that*!"

Layla felt her stomach begin to churn.

"Now let's see," Michelle continued, "I have to think like a candidate. I have to dress more classy, be seen at all the right places, get a new boyfriend and, oh, what else? Oh yeah, get better grades. Oh, but of course you'll help me with that last one..."

Layla knew that she would have to endure at least ten more minutes of this excited banter without a break. She felt like setting the phone down and letting Michelle chatter on as much as she wanted to while she went and got a drink, but then she thought the better of it, realizing she would have to provide the occasional "Hmm's," and "Uh huh's" to avoid offending the newest princess of the town.

The one-sided conversation actually went on for another half an hour before Michelle interrupted herself and cried out, "Oh, my phone beeped. I got a call on the other line. One second..." *Click.*

Layla, who in the past would have been annoyed by being made to wait, was thankful for the break. It gave her time to decipher all the mixed up gibberish that was heaved upon her. She tried to pick apart the elements of Michelle's excited stream of babble but came away without the one thing she had hoped to hear: that Michelle acknowledged putting Layla's name on the sign up board and that she was sorry for doing it.

"Well," mused Layla, "Michelle's so excited now she won't even *remember* doing it. I mean, what does she think she's *running for*?" Layla paused and then said out loud, "*President* or something?"

After a few minutes on hold, Layla figured it was safe enough to hang up. She could always say, "*We got cut off.*" Besides, if Michelle really had anything more important to say she would call back. That, of course, was the one possibility that Layla hoped wouldn't happen this time. This whole "Popularity Contest" thing was going to put a crack in their friendship, as it had already started to do, and Layla knew it.

Hoping to further drown her sorrows in homework, for one pain can assuage another, or so the saying goes, she sat down at her desk wearily and began to scribble the heading on her next homework paper. Just then the phone rang again. "*Oh great.*" Layla sighed as she rolled her eyes hopelessly.

"Yes." She answered languidly into the transmitter.

"*Assalamu 'alaykum, Layla,*" a familiar and *welcome* voice announced.

Layla smiled when she realized who it was. "*Wa 'alaykum assalam.* Rayhanna! How are you?"

"I'm doing okay, *alhumdulillah*. It's been a while since we've talked and I wanted to see how you were doing."

Layla felt some of the burden lift from her mind as she strolled over to her bed and leaned back comfortably on her fluffy pillow. Rayhanna was her friend from weekend school at the *Masjid*. She lived in another town, though, so they really didn't have any contact other than four times a month for a few hours each time.

"Well," replied Layla, "I'm doing okay, too, I guess. What are you up to?"

"I'm just doing my science homework, but I got bored of rocks and how they're made and I thought to myself, *'Who can cheer me up more than my rock and pebble homework?'* and *boom* - I thought of you!"

"Gee, thanks." Layla laughed. "Hey, isn't your older sister, Fatimah, getting married next month?"

"Yeah," Rayhanna answered excitedly. "*Alhumdulillah*! I'll finally get a break from hearing her brag about Kamran. That's all I've been hearing about lately: Kamran is *so* great. Kamran is *so* handsome. Kamran is *so* this and *so* that. Let me tell you. I hope I never get married if that's what it does to your brain!"

Layla laughed. She was so thankful for this light-hearted break from all her troubles at school. She wished again that all her friends could be *normal* girls like Rayhanna. Whenever she talked to her friends from weekend school, she didn't have to worry about hearing the latest on whose boyfriend dumped who, whose party had liquor, whose clothes were so tacky or who's more popular than so and so. With these friends it was a different world completely. It was honest and *pure*.

"So how's school going for you?" Rayhanna asked.

"Oh, *fine*." Layla replied. "You know - the usual hassles."

"I know how it is. Yesterday someone tried to pull my *hijab* off in the hall - *again*."

"Really? What did you do?"

"What could I do? It was one of those shrimpy freshmen boys. I think his name was Mark Stimson or something. He'd better watch out, though, or next time I'll stomp him flat!"

"Oh yeah, I know about wanting to stomp somebody." Layla offered excitedly, "My so-called friend, Michelle, entered my name in the "Who's the Most Popular Kid in School" contest. What am I going to do? I'm the *least* popular kid in school. I only have a couple of friends there and even then they're a bit iffy. Now I'm afraid everyone's going to laugh at me tomorrow when word gets around that my name will be on the ballot."

"Wow! That's a tough one." Rayhanna intoned sympathetically. "Did you confront her about it yet?"

"No," Layla sighed. "I didn't see any point. She probably thought she was doing me a favor or something. I figured it wasn't worth making a big scene about. Having her as a friend is the one thing that keeps me from falling off the social ladder altogether."

"Couldn't you just take your name off?"

"No. This stuck-up girl named Linda said I couldn't. She's on the Student Council and they're guarding that sign-up sheet like it was a gold mine or something. Besides, even if I tried to erase my name secretly, They'd probably start teasing me about being a chicken or something."

"So what are you going to do?"

"I don't know." Layla intoned. "I guess I'll just take it day-by-day and see what happens. Hey, a hundred years from now who will care?" She added in a hopeful yet lilting voice.

"I'll make a *du'a* for you." Rayhanna offered. "Oh, I gotta' go. My Mom's calling me for 'Isha prayer."

"I'd better go do my *wudu*, too. My mom'll probably call me any minute, as well."

"I'll see you next weekend."

"*Insha'llah.*"

"*Assalamu 'alaykum.*"

"*Wa 'alaykum assalam.*"

Layla hung up the phone. She felt a little bit better. At least she knew that she had real friends who understood her and felt the same way about life that she did.

"O Allah," Layla softly said aloud, "Help me out on this one, *please*." Then she went to wash up for the night prayer.

6

The morning was going fairly well, or so Layla thought, as she trundled from class to class, trying her best to ignore the stares and whispers. Discrimination and prejudice she knew well and she had developed some very sophisticated internal defenses for dealing with them. Perhaps, she mused, she could apply some of those inner blocks to this new situation facing her.

Ducking absentmindedly into the bathroom between English and science classes, she began to consider more closely her own remarkable strengths. She began to feel that maybe she could apply those same techniques for self-preservation to dealing with this new situation.

Suddenly, an angry voice called out from behind her. "Hey, *Deen*!" Still think you're gonna' win?"

Layla turned around from the white porcelain sink and looked right into the glowering face of Shamika Thompkins, a tall ebony girl with a strikingly plaited hair weave and a strong, well-etched face. Beside her stood two of her equally tall and very tough looking friends.

"Oh great," Layla thought to herself, "My tombstone will read, *Pulverized in the second floor bathroom*.'"

"Nobody goes up against *Shamika* and has a chance." The obviously annoyed and chic girl announced with a swish of her imposingly long index finger.

"Tha's right," one of the girls standing besides her cheered, quite enthusiastically Layla thought.

"You'd best not be thinking of crossing me, *girlfriend*." Shamika went on. "I *am* the queen of this school and nobody gets in my way."

The thought flashed through Layla's mind that all popular people everywhere must be self-absorbed jerks, but she was quickly brought back to the heat of the moment when Shamika raised her manicured finger once more and backed her prey up against the mirrored wall in between two of the sinks. "And furthermore," Shamika went on, "I don't want to see any posters with *your* name on them in any hallway where *mine* are."

Layla felt the pressure of her assailer and almost crumbled under her crushing psychological assault. But then something happened, something that surprised even Layla, herself. She stiffened her back and angrily shot back saying, "I didn't write my name on the sign-in sheet and I don't want to be in this stupid contest but Linda Patterson won't let me out. I think it's the dumbest idea ever."

"*Is that so*?" Shamika exclaimed, tilting her head slightly in surprise. "Well, *Deen,* you won't win anyway. I thought I'd come by and warn you just in case you was thinkin' you were better than everybody else just 'cause you wear that rag on your head and all."

"That's my *hijab*." Layla protested indignantly. "It's not a *rag*. I don't wear it to make people think I'm good. I only wear it because God gave it as a shield to women for their respect and protection." Layla began to feel a little stronger now that the issue was moving to familiar territory. She was used to talking along these lines.

"What do you mean *respect and protection*? The only thing God gave women was hotness, and we use it to get what we want." Shamika noted wryly, as her two friends bobbed their heads in agreement. One of the girls, a thinly built track runner, pursed her lips while the other girl, a stockier teen with her hair in a tight corn roll sucked her teeth condescendingly.

40

"Since when does using your looks to achieve your goals mean anything? Don't some people use your looks against you, saying they don't like your color? Don't the boys always come when a girl looks good and then leave when her looks fade? What about the real person inside? Doesn't that count for anything? Are we just a bunch of pretty airheads using the worst qualities in men just to get them to give us stuff? And then when we're old and alone what will we have - a broken life filled with false dreams?"

Layla's impassioned plea, a mixture of what she had learned in weekend school and her own thoughts on the subject over many years caught Shamika and her friends off guard.

This allowed Layla to press ahead and take the topic back to herself. She pointed to her *hijab* and explained, "When I wear this scarf, covering over my looks, people can't judge me by my appearance only. They have to judge me by my intelligence, character and personality. And when I wear it, it helps keep the boys from staring at me in bad ways. This scarf forces people to deal with me on a level beyond my physical looks. It says, 'Hey, there's a real person here. Deal with her as an equal.'"

Shamika paused, stunned for a moment. Layla gritted her teeth to soften the blow she felt sure was coming, but then Shamika laughed and swung her hands in front of her as her girlfriends giggled and tried to soak in what they had just heard. Then, staring at Layla with a half-cocked smile on her face, she said, "Girlfriend, I can dig that. Men *are dogs*."

Her two friends nodded eagerly in agreement, "That's right. Boys treat us *lousy*," one of them intoned. Shamika paused again and it seemed as if she was remembering something that had happened long ago. "You're the real deal," she exclaimed. "Hey," she said as she waved her finger in a flourish, "I'll see ya' 'round."

Layla exhaled the deep breath she had been holding in as Shamika and her two friends left the bathroom. She was about to begin pondering the weird experience she had just had when she heard some hard coughing coming from one of the stalls in the back section of the large girl's bathroom. She was about to ignore it and leave, thankful to have escaped certain doom, when the coughing became even harder.

"Are you all right in there?" She called out to the occupant of the stall as she moved into the long section of brightly colored green stall doors. There was no reply.

She discreetly and slowly bent her head down to look at the floor under the open bottom walls of the stalls. There she saw the chunky combat boots. She instantly knew who was there. Kelly Spitz. As she stood up straight she noticed the faint smell of a burning, smoky thing, almost like rotten ammonia.

"That is one *nasty* smell," she thought to herself.

The sudden flush of a toilet startled her and before she could react, the door to the stall in front of her flung open and a puff of unworldly smoke came billowing out around her. Then she saw Kelly, standing there with a large silver linked chain necklace hanging around her neck. A faint cloud of acrid smoke hung around her head almost giving her hair a gray halo.

"What're you lookin' at?" She snarled, and before Layla could answer, Kelly pushed her way past her and darted out the door into the crowded hallway.

Layla smelled the smoke again and her nostrils curled in revulsion. She had been in school long enough to know that the bathrooms were often filled with students smoking cigarettes and many a time she entered into a foul den of fog and other weird odors which otherwise should have been a clean, well-kept public facility. But this smoke smelled different, it was from no cigarette Layla ever smelled.

Thinking quickly, Layla exited the bathroom, lest any of that strange smoke get in her clothes and cause her to reek the rest of the day. But what was Kelly doing? Layla wondered, as she went to her next class. It seemed like at every turn that she was abusing herself in one way or another.

She had only known about Kelly for seven months or so. Up until now, Layla had always felt a strange kind of affinity for the obviously troubled girl whom everyone avoided and made fun of. After all, this is sort of how Layla was treated at times. But Layla never got the chance to know her or talk to her because Kelly always kept to herself and avoided other students. She was also guilty of skipping classes all the time.

Layla would have been tempted to tell on her for smoking in the bathroom if this was elementary school, but it wasn't. A kid who breaks the rules is often considered cool and daring in junior high society. Sometimes it seemed to Layla that the more despicable a teen was the more in demand he or she would be in the social circles of the 'in' crowd. Although Kelly wasn't in demand or anything, on account of her overly rude attitude and mean demeanor, she did have a sort of notoriety.

Besides, anyone who told on another student was labeled a traitor and called names such as *Narc*, *Rat* or even worse. Layla had enough troubles on her hands already to make her want to avoid having to endure such humiliation for the sake of telling on Kelly Spitz - or anyone else for that matter.

She again became distracted as she entered her fifth period class and took her seat near the back left side of the room. All the popular kids sat on the right side of the room and often threw paper wads and other things at the rest of the class when the teacher wasn't looking.

"Well," thought Layla, as a paper ball whizzed by the unlucky girl in front of her, "another day in the war zone."

7

The next several days passed uneventfully for Layla. Michelle, who was now absorbed in building alliances in the social circuit, hadn't called at all, and except for another call from her good friend, Rayhanna, Layla was pretty much left alone. This unexpected break from useless talking on the phone with Michelle made her feel somehow *free*.

It was a strange feeling and the more time she had to think the more she wondered if it was really worth it to be friends with Michelle. Layla was hard-pressed to think of one good benefit she actually got out of the relationship. Her evening musings were interrupted, however, by the ringing of the phone next to her bed.

"Yes?" Layla stated firmly.

"Oh my God!" The voice on the other end shouted so loudly that Layla had to move the phone away from ear a little bit. "I'm so excited!" The voice continued.

Layla sighed and rolled her eyes. It was Michelle.

"You'll never guess what happened. You know how the ballots are going to be given out next week for voting who's the most popular?" Before Layla could answer, Michelle continued. "Well, the Student Council decided to arrange an assembly after lunch this Friday so that all the candidates could have a chance to speak and tell the student body why they should be picked the most popular!"

Layla almost dropped the phone out of her hand, "What? I, uh..."

"That's so *awesome*! This will give me a chance to get one up on Linda Patterson and her goonie-squad. I can go straight to the student population all at once and win their hearts and minds for my cause."

Layla stiffened when she heard the word *cause* being used for such a petty thing.

"So what should I wear?" Michelle stammered excitedly. "Should I go conservative or go for something *wild*?"

Layla shuddered at the thought of *Michelle* and *wild* together in the same sentence. Before she could start chattering again, Layla connected with the nervous feeling in the pit of her stomach and asked, "Do all the candidates have to speak at the assembly?"

"Well, of course silly."

"But I'm a candidate, as if you didn't already know."

"Yeah, that's right! I saw your name on the list. I wonder *who* nominated *you*? See I told you lots of other people liked you."

Layla gritted her teeth and thought silently about how much she wished she could say, *"Yeah, I bet you saw my name there - and you're the one who wrote it*!"

Choking down the urge to chew her friend out royally, Layla continued as calmly as possible, "So *what*? Am I supposed to get up there and talk to a bunch of dorks and tell 'em why I want to a win a contest I don't want to win and that I didn't enter it and that I think it's stupid?"

"Oh, *lighten up*, girl." Michelle chided playfully. "No one will be paying much attention to you anyway because all the tension will be on the real contest between me and Linda Patterson."

"Thanks a lot." Layla muttered.

"And don't think of not speaking," Michelle continued, "because if you don't it will look really bad for you. Imagine what the other students will say about you if you chicken out?"

Michelle then bantered on mindlessly about what she was going to say, what shoes she was going to wear and how great it would be when all the students cheered her in front of Linda Patterson.

Then, just as Layla had successfully almost tuned her out of her active mind, Michelle suddenly announced, "Oh, there's the beep. Must be another call coming in. Gotta' go, Bye."

A resounding '*click*' ended the hurricane swirling around Layla's tired ear. Before returning the phone to its cradle, Layla froze for a moment and felt that events were spinning way out of control. It was time, she felt, to do the unthinkable. It was time to break down and ask her brother Ahmad's advice.

8

"Hey, Ahmad!" the coach yelled. "C'mon, practice is over, way over, and I gotta' get home some time in this lifetime."

Ahmad, who had asked the coach to stay late and give him some pointers on his hurdling technique, turned his head as he leapt over a three-footer and nodded affirmatively. He returned sprinting to the beginning of the course and crouched down in the starting position in the center lane. "One last run!" he called excitedly as he suddenly burst forward in a spontaneous rush of energy. He quickly rose to a running position and leapt with all his power over the first hurdle that confronted him. His technique was flawless.

The same effort was put into the next nine hurdles, though on the last, probably out of sheer exhaustion, he nicked the top of the white wooden rail. He slowed his running pace to a jog and then headed over towards the direction of the track coach, Mr. Sanchez.

"Okay," Ahmad huffed as he neared the astonished man, "let's call it a day."

"Let me tell you," the coach said, as he lifted his already packed duffel bag, "any coach would be proud to have you run track, but then again, it would have to be an over-time coach who's willing to *live* at the sports field."

"Well," Ahmad chuckled, running his fingers through his forehead, "I could set up a bed for you under the bleachers."

"No thanks." he laughed. "I prefer my nice, warm house. By the way, I think you missed clearing that last hurdle."

Ahmad nodded affirmatively.

"You were probably tired, though. Your teammates left over an hour ago and you kept at it. You must want to win pretty badly."

"I just want to be the best. I've learned there's no point in settling for second when if you just tried harder you could probably succeed."

"Well," the coach answered, tilting his head, "sometimes second ain't that bad if you have no control over your competition."

Ahmad, who suddenly remembered a saying of his main role model, Prophet Muhammad, peace be on him, replied, "I guess winning and losing isn't always in our hands anyway. God has the final say."

The coach thought for a moment about how mature Ahmad was for his age and then wished all his athletes were so clear of mind. "See you next Wednesday," he waved as he passed through the gates into the parking lot.

Ahmad waved and then walked out to his own car. The drive home would give him the chance to think about the lesson he learned from the coach and how it made him remember to be a better Muslim.

"Ahmad?" Layla called out from outside his door.

"Yeah," a muffled voice called back.

"Can I come in? I want to ask you something."

"Sure, the door is open."

Layla knew the door was always open, for Ahmad never shut out his two sisters. Although it was mostly Hafsa who came in and interacted with him these past two years, Layla still knew she was welcome.

Ahmad was working on his chemistry homework but quickly put down his sheet of chemical reaction data and turned his swivel chair around from his desk to face his sister. Layla sat on the edge of his bed and crossed her legs. She sat silently for a moment.

"What can I do for 'ya?" Ahmad asked.

"Ahmad," she began, "I've got sort of a problem and I want to know what you think."

"Sure. What's it about? You need help on math or something?"

"No, not really. My homework is going fine. It's, well, it's something that's going on at school.

"Is someone bothering you? If they are I'll…"

"Oh no," Layla interrupted, "It's not like that. It's really different. Ahmad, when you were in junior high, did they have any contests or stuff?"

"You mean like raffles or sports competitions? Sure. I always entered them because…"

"No, I mean like social stuff, like who's the best student, who should lead the pep squad. You know - contests where people either like you or they don't and the results are announced for everyone to see."

Ahmad relaxed his shoulders and leaned back in his padded dark swivel chair. "Well, now that you mention it, there was that one thing they did when I was a freshmen. They called it the Most Likely to Succeed contest. The kids took a poll and wrote the names of anyone they thought would be rich and famous when they grew up. As a joke, a lot of kids also wrote who they thought would be a homeless beggar right on the bottom of the ballot. It was for the yearbook so it was kinda' all in fun. Mostly it was for the older grades. I thought it was dumb, though."

Layla sat up straighter. "Did anyone write your name on the ballot? What did you think? Were you made fun of?"

"Whoa," Ahmad raised his hands in front of him. "No one knew me back then, thank Allah. I would hate to have people writing what they thought about me in a poll."

"You don't even know the *half* of it." Layla thought to herself.

"What would you have done if they *did* include you one way or the other?" Layla asked as she picked up a football that her foot found while tapping nervously.

"I wouldn't care." Ahmad said matter-of-factly. "Let them write whatever they want. It's not who I am. Allah knows me and who cares what anyone else thinks of me?"

"But how would you act in school if something like that did happen?" Layla asked, rolling the football back on the floor, trying not to appear too eager for an answer.

"I'd act just the same. Hey, whether they think I'm a hobo or a popular guy shouldn't affect what I do or what I think about myself. If I let it affect me then I'm giving other people power over my feelings and that's not something I want to do."

Layla sat in silence for a minute, fidgeting with the football and other sports equipment on the floor at the end of Ahmad's bed. Something he said made sense but she wasn't sure how it would work for her. Suddenly she stood up and said, "Thanks, Ahmad. You've been a big help."

"No problem. Are you sure that's all you needed?"

"Yeah," Layla replied, as she stood up to go.

Ahmad nodded and then sighed as he swiveled back around to face his desk and the work still awaiting him there.

Layla went back to her room and spent the rest of the evening pondering the advice she got from her brother. She was certainly thankful that she didn't have to reveal anything overt about her situation to get it. Figuring out what she would have to do now, however, occupied her thoughts deep into the night.

9

Layla ate her breakfast in silence. Her father had already left for work and her mother was busy getting Hafsa's lunch ready. Although she slept at least half the night, the other half was spent in a nervous series of gymnastics under the covers. She just couldn't seem to get comfortable. Of course the problem wasn't her mattress, though, but her inability to take her mind off of the unreal nightmare she had inadvertently stumbled into. When her corn flakes were finished, she lazily dragged herself without a sound into the first floor bathroom to put her *hijab* on.

Looking into the mirror, she saw herself for what seemed like the first time in a long time. Staring back at her was a girl unsure of herself and how others saw her. What if she *were* popular? How would her life be different then?

The thought crossed her mind and grew slowly into an aching question that seemed to take on a life of its own. Without realizing it, she began to slip into a surreal daydream in which she imagined herself walking through the hallway of her school, waving to everybody and seeing all the other students smiling at her and calling out her name. Her locker and all the space around it was the focal point of popularity. All the coolest and prettiest girls pushed and shoved each other to be closest to her and the boys treated her like a queen.

Her clothes would reflect the latest trends: DKNY, Steve Madden, J. Crew, and all the rest. Her teachers loved her and gave her encouragement and preferential treatment. No party would be complete without her on the top of the guest list. "How much better would life be if I *were* popular?" Layla mused in her trance.

The vision soon began to take hold of Layla physically. She felt glued to the image in her mind's eye as the alternative picture of her life as it might have been invaded her heart and emotions. She even found herself beginning to resent the fact that she had to wear a head covering when all the other girls were able to run with their hair flowing free, braided, curled, permed or gelled. Layla imagined herself walking in front of all the other students without her *hijab*, her beautiful hair framing her pretty face. People would admire her. The girls wouldn't tease her. The boys would look at her.

With strange abruptness, however, Layla's daydreaming took on a decidedly darker tone. It was almost as if a cloud descended upon the fringes of her mind and enveloped her in a thick, dense haze. She felt a twinge of anxiety and a weird transformation materialized before her eyes.

She saw the beautiful people of her school in the hallways, waving, but their faces were beginning to change, to stretch and contort. Shifting out of proportion, their pristine beauty began to turn into ugliness; wrinkly and deformed. Full lips turned to dark holes on their faces. Eyes disappeared leaving empty, cold sockets. Layla felt goose bumps travel up her spine but she couldn't break the force of this increasingly ominous vision.

The scenery then abruptly changed as well to a party and everyone was dancing to loud music all over the living room of someone's house. She couldn't make out anyone in particular. It was all just mindless swaying to a never-ending beat. The people seemed trapped in their rhythm and couldn't escape. They looked like they were happy, holding drinks - alcoholic - yet they had an incredible sadness in their eyes.

A flash of light replaced the wild party with an icily still room. It was a mess with papers and bottles all over the floor. There was no sound, no movement, just quiet. People were lying around on the carpet, the couch and in the hallways.

Layla heard a girl crying. She was sitting in a corner by the stairs and weeping profusely. Her hair was a mess and her makeup was smeared around her lips and under her eyes. She looked nothing less than *broken*. A boy came out of what looked like the bathroom, holding his head and moaning in pain. The music had stopped at some point earlier but the profound sadness that remained was as intense as the noise had been before. The girl picked up a bottle and drank greedily, coughing in between breaths.

Layla stared at her intently, noting how she clutched her side, and an overpowering white haze quickly began forming at the edges of her vision, closing in and down, obscuring the face of the girl. Before the blinding white fazed into nothingness, however, something oddly familiar in the girl's face made Layla marvel, but she couldn't put her finger on it.

Layla suddenly found herself back again in the hall of her school and the popular girls were all around her, crying and wailing; asking for help. Behind them were a lot of mean looking boys, looking at them in frighteningly wicked ways, eyes radiating fire. Layla could see their faces; their darkly ominous intentions. She felt those boys staring at her, too, with her beautiful hair and trendy clothes. They were looking, moving closer like hunters; their teeth flashed hungrily.

Then she saw the girl who had been crying at the party. She wanted to say something to comfort her but as she placed her hand under the chin of the girl to lift her head, she was horrified to see her own face, staring back at her with smudged makeup and eyeliner. Suddenly she was back in the still room where people were still passed out after the raucous party. She saw the girl crying. She was the girl. She sat in a dark corner crying, "No! No! No!" She cried out in the loudest voice she could muster. "No!"

There was a banging sound, a pounding sound. The room began to spin, echoing voices became screams in her head. Faces leered down at her in the school hall; loomed over her. She couldn't run. She couldn't move. Heartbeats raced faster and faster and the pounding didn't seem to stop.

The pounding was in her head, in her heart, in her hands when suddenly she slipped forward from where her hands had been clutching the edge of the sink and bumped her face on the mirror, waking her from her nightmarish daydream. Locking eyes with the bruised face in the glass, *her face*, Layla panted for breath and struggled to keep her balance. For a moment she couldn't hear her heartbeat.

She was just about to let her terrified senses begin their slow return to normalcy when a voice called out, causing her to jump in surprise.

"Let's go!" A voice screamed from outside the bathroom door. The pounding she heard she now recognized as the impatient knocking of Hafsa's little fists. "I'm gonna' tell mom if you don't come out! C'mon! You're scaring me! Layla, Come out!"

Layla paused for a second to get her bearings. She looked around. She was safe in her own house. The stillness in the air was only broken by more pounding outside the door.

"I'll be out in a minute!" she called out hoarsely, gaining her a temporary reprieve. Looking into the mirror, she noticed a reddish bump on her cheek from her accident a moment before. Layla knew what she really wanted now. She didn't want to be like *the crowd*. She didn't want their sadness, their parties, their alcohol and drugs or their values. She wanted to be *free*. She wanted to be a Muslim. She wanted to be who she was: Layla, simply Layla, the Muslim girl with the good heart and sincere smile.

Layla finished fixing her *hijab* over her hair, with a new kind of determination in her fingers. She looked again at the red bump on her cheek. It would be a small bruise that would last for days. But it also meant more for her, she realized, as she studied its outline. It would be her badge of truth; a lesson learned. She almost wished it would last longer to remind her about who she was meant to be. After a quick final adjustment, she took a deep, centering breath and then opened the bathroom door and prepared herself to meet the day, whatever it held for her.

"Hey *Lula*!" a voice shouted from somewhere behind her in the crowded hallway at school. Layla rolled her eyes in quiet desperation as she turned to see Linda Patterson prancing by with her groupies. "How are you gonna' convince the student body to vote for you on Friday? Are you gonna' rub your nose on the ground or something and beg them?"

Linda's five friends, all of them slender and pretty, burst out in laughter. Early in the school year when the time for the noon prayer would fall within school hours, Layla used to go out into the courtyard in front of the school and perform her religious duties. Although she tried to pray discreetly behind a bench or a tree, she had been frequently seen bowing and prostrating as Muslims do in prayer. It was, much to her chagrin, another source of ridicule from the more prejudiced students. After a while she had gotten used to finding empty classrooms to pray.

Layla bit her teeth together and looked slightly over Linda's shoulder to the wall behind her, trying real hard not to say something mean in return. She began counting silently, "One. Two. Three..."

Linda laughed harder and one of her friends threw a candy wrapper at Layla. Other students stopped to watch as Linda's "gang" surrounded the hapless girl and kept on taunting her. "Rag-head!" one girl shouted, to the glee of her friends. "Camel-jockey!" called another. Layla had undergone this kind of name calling before but this was the first time an actual mob formed around her. She froze and pressed her back against the lockers. She was about to say something in her defense, however useless, when someone from behind the now swollen crowd yelled out, "Hey! Patterson! What are you, a freak or something? Leave the girl alone!"

Just then Shamika Thompkins pushed through the crowd and confronted Linda face-to-face. Her two tall (and tough looking) friends quickly took up positions behind her. Linda was shocked for a second because no one had ever stood up to her before.

Shamika glared menacingly as Linda, who quickly surmised that she would lose face if she backed down, shifted her stance and put her hands on her hips defiantly. "What's wrong with you?" Linda asked in a wry voice. "You like rag-heads or something?"

By now word of the potential fight swept through the hallways and students rushed to get into the circle of spectators. Some were calling out, "Cat-fight! Cat-fight!" Shamika raised her voice over the noise and pointed her finger in Linda's face, "Don't tell me who I can and can't like. This girl's done nothing to you and you're always dissing her. You just leave her alone or..."

Just then, the assistant principal, Mr. Gottbaum, burst through the crowd and yelled, "Hold it right there! There'll be no fighting in this school. You, you and..." he pointed to a friend of Linda's first, then Shamika and finally moved his finger slowly in the air as he searched for someone else to punish.

His gaze fell upon Layla, who had been glued to the locker behind her. He thrust his finger in her direction and said, "And *you*. To the office. Now!"

"What about Linda?" Shamika called out loudly. "Ain't she gonna' go too?"

"I saw you three fighting, not her." Mr. Gottbaum sneered. Linda smirked triumphantly, safe in the knowledge that her status protected her well. The fact that one of her friends would sacrifice herself for her only emboldened her sense of power.

Layla was about to protest as well, but the look on Mr. Gottbaum's face said it all: he wasn't *even* going to listen to *her*. She meekly took her position in the line of doom as the three girls marched towards the office, Mr. Gottbaum in tow.

The crowd melted away as the buzzer for the next class went off without taking any notice of what happened in the hallways it diligently watched over.

10

"...and furthermore, both of you will have to sign up for an after school community service program. If I catch you causing trouble again you'll receive an even greater penalty, perhaps even suspension. Do I make myself clear?"

Shamika rolled her eyes and mumbled an apparently well-rehearsed, "Yeah, sure. Whatever you say."

Layla, not believing the unfairness of what was happening to her, nodded her head silently in resignation. She would've protested, called for justice, but the man before her refused to even hear their side of the story.

Layla angrily concluded that she shouldn't waste any of her valuable breath for Mr. Gottbaum's sake. The final result: Gottbaum let Linda's friend go with a half-hearted warning, never punished Linda at all, gave Layla and Shamika two days detention and now was forcing them to sign up for community service two days a week after school for a month. Layla was pretty sure that she wouldn't have a problem explaining what happened to her parents, but the injustice of it all was unnerving to all of her moral sensibilities.

What was worse was that she knew she couldn't do anything about it. Gottbaum dismissed them and, with Shamika in the lead, they filed out of the assistant principal's office into the large school office waiting area.

"Listen, Shamika, I'm sorry this happ..." Layla began to say, but a quickly raised hand from Shamika silenced her.

"Don't worry yourself about it." She said. "Gottbaum and me – let's just say we go way back. He's punished me so many times for stuff I didn't do that I just stopped countin'."

Layla adjusted the ends of her scarf over her shoulders and smiled, "Thanks for sticking up for me back there. I was really scared the way they backed me into a corner. I don't know what I ever did to Linda to make her hate me so."

"It don't take nothin' for someone to hate. I'm black so I know that real good. Anyway, after a while you get used to it so you don't expect nothin' good from nobody. I just got mad when I saw that stuck up girl trying to pick a fight with you. She's bigger than you and that ain't fair."

"Does this mean we're disqualified from the Popularity Contest?" Layla asked hopefully. "I mean, look, we've been given detention and community service. That's *gotta'* mean we're out."

"The rules don't say nothin' about getting kicked out of the contest and don't you say a word to nobody 'bout it. I want to win this thing to show that high nose girl that I got what it takes to win. Besides, I'm naturally beautiful anyway, so me winning is the only possible outcome." Shamika raised her hands to frame the edge of her face as she said the last line and then pranced out of the office into the empty hallway.

Layla sighed to herself, "Oh great. Now I can't look for a way out or *Shamika* will get mad at me." She stood there for a moment in reflective silence and walked over to the main desk of the office where a number of sign up sheets were hanging around the long brownish-colored counter top. Behind the counter were several desks and filing cabinets. A student helper, a nerdy boy named Jason, came up and asked, "What can I do for you?"

Layla sighed again and said, "I need to sign up for an after school community service program."

The intern smirked as if he had been through this procedure before and pointed to a clipboard to his right. "Here is the list." He said. "When you find the program you like, write your name and the code number on the sign-up sheet underneath.

Layla took the clipboard in her hands as the intern scurried away. Before her was an alphabetical list of programs students could *volunteer* for. Well, in her case, it would definitely be *involuntary*.

As she scrolled her finger down the titles she saw two that interested her slightly: daycare story time and CPR. It might be hard to get to the district daycare center, she thought, because she didn't have a car and Ahmad wasn't always home after school. "CPR it is." She muttered and signed her name in the next available slot. The class was held in the school building so she wouldn't have a problem getting there.

Before leaving the office she took a pass from the secretary, pondered one last time over the unfairness of what she had just experienced, and steeled herself to survive the rest of the day.

"*Assalamu 'alaykum*, Rayhanna." Layla said as she heard the phone on the other end get picked up.

"*Wa 'alaykum assalam*, Layla. How are you?"

"Not good. It's been a real weird week and it just keeps getting worse."

"What happened?"

Layla rolled over on her bed and put her feet up on the wall. "I got in trouble at school today. I mean, I didn't do anything and now I have two days of detention, community service *and* I'm trapped for good in the Popularity Contest."

"Wow!" Rayhanna intoned, sympathetically. "How did all *that* happen?"

Layla told Rayhanna everything that occurred and when she finished, she gave a lamented summary, saying, "Look at this. I had to sign up Michelle to keep her as a friend. Then she double-crossed me and put my name on the sign-up board. Then I got cornered in the hall, sent to the office, punished for nothing and now I can't even ask to be kicked out of the contest or Shamika will get mad at me for jeopardizing her chances of winning."

"Boy," Rayhanna exclaimed, "it can't get any worse than that. When someone said junior high was the pits, they really meant it. Do you have any ideas about what to do? What did your mom say?"

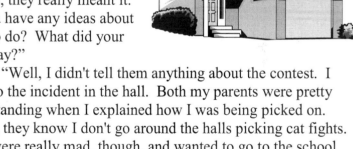

"Well, I didn't tell them anything about the contest. I stuck to the incident in the hall. Both my parents were pretty understanding when I explained how I was being picked on. C'mon, they know I don't go around the halls picking cat fights. They were really mad, though, and wanted to go to the school and complain, but I begged and begged them not to. I mean, that would just make things worse."

"Tell me about it. Once my dad complained to a teacher about giving me an unfair grade on my report card and after that the teacher wouldn't call on me again in class to answer questions or to read."

"I wish I were ignored by my teachers," Layla said softly as she glanced over at her desk. To her immense satisfaction it was completely empty. She had been able to complete all her homework during detention that day. Now there was only one day of it left.

She sort of liked not having to bring anything home for once but she also disliked having to call Ahmad at his school during practice to come pick her up from an official punishment. Although he wouldn't ever say anything about it, she hated to bother him for that kind of reason.

"Oh, Layla," Rayhanna exclaimed with a concerned tone of voice, "isn't tomorrow the day you have to speak in front of the whole school?"

Layla's heart fell flat in her chest as the pile of worries she had momentarily forgotten escaped from the prison of disliked memories locked deep within her brain. "Oh yeah," she answered in a lilting voice.

"What are you going to say?"

"I don't know. I asked my brother for advice, in a round about way, but he still doesn't know I'm in the contest. I really can't think of anything to say. I mean, I really don't want to speak at all but if I don't it would be even more embarrassing. The last thing I need is to be laughed at for chickening out. I'm really stuck here and I don't know what I did to deserve this."

"Do I detect a pattern here?" Rayhanna announced suddenly. "Do you remember what we learned in weekend school last year, you know, about *Qadr*?"

Layla thought for a moment and then the memories of last year's classes flooded back into her mind. Their teacher, sister Nadia, was a really cool lady. She made the religion class on the weekend truly interesting, which was a pleasant change from all the boring teachers she usually had there.

One of her lessons was on the topic of *Qadr*, or *Measurement*: everything that happens to you is *measured out* by Allah, in other words, your tests and challenges are something that you just *can't* avoid. Sometimes you're just meant to go through certain hardships to make you a better person in the end. On a merciful note, sister Nadia explained,

Allah wouldn't burden a soul beyond what it could handle.

Though you can't stop all those challenges, she also had said, you do have the choice in how you *feel* about the events of your life and whether you are thankful or spiteful to God. So the basic lesson was that you can't stop events from engulfing you but you can manage your own feelings.

"Do you think all of this is your *Qadr*?" Rayhanna asked.

"Well, it certainly looks like it." Layla replied thoughtfully. Somehow, putting an Islamic label on her problems made her feel better, as if it was now more familiar or manageable.

Islam was a subject she knew. If she applied what she knew to this whole mess maybe an answer would come as well. It was as if she had reached the end of a tunnel with no doors and suddenly someone opened a crack for her to slip through.

"*So*, if I can't change the situation..." Layla said in a different tone of voice.

"Then you can change how you *feel* about it!" Rayhanna finished emphatically.

"Well," Layla sighed, "*that's* easier said than done. I still don't want to speak tomorrow at lunch."

"But you're a good speaker. Think of all those speeches you gave in the *Masjid*. You even won the speech competition a few years back, remember."

Memories of speaking in front of a large crowd of bored kids flashed in front of her mind. "You're right," she answered. "I'm not really worried about being *able* to speak. I just don't know what I'm going to say. It's not like I can stand up there and talk about Abu Bakr or Hajj or something. They're all non-Muslims. They have different concerns and interests."

"Find something they *are* interested in and talk about that. I mean, think about it: you *don't* want to win, right?"

"No, I certainly do *not* want to win any *popularity contest*."

"See, Layla. If you don't want to win, it doesn't matter what you talk about it. Give'm some *da'wah* and good advice about life and show 'em that you're the sincere one with the good values. It'll make the other candidates look like airheads. Then, even though you're trying not to win, when it's all over people may respect you more. You know, turn a bad situation into a better one."

Layla thought about that for a moment. She quickly began to consider what she could say. She immediately realized, however, that she wouldn't be able to concentrate on her conversation with Rayhanna any longer so she bid her *salams* to her friend and hung up the phone.

After she finished the night prayer she went to bed and ran over different topics in her head. Maybe she could use this whole thing to her advantage. She could show the school what she was all about. She *did* have the power to change how she felt about all of this. Maybe Allah was giving her an opportunity and not a curse.

For the first time Layla *actually* began to understand what *Qadr* really meant. She drifted off to sleep some hours later and slept a little more peacefully than she had done in a long while.

11

Layla waited on the curb in silence. The sun was just beginning to rise over the horizon, casting a pale light over the dew soaked trees and rooftops of her neighborhood. She inhaled a heavy breath and savored the cool crisp air, scented of plants and flowers.

A faint breeze rose in an unseen corner causing some leaves to rustle past her, swirling by her feet momentarily before rushing off to some other curb. She considered them bemusedly, wondering at how easy their journey this day would be compared to hers. They had nothing more to worry about now since their job of producing energy for their host tree was done.

For Layla there would be no such easy escape.   It was Friday. D-Day, short for *Do or Die day*, as far as she was concerned, as this was the day when all the contestants in the Popularity Contest had to address the student body.

Of course, she planned everything she *did* have control over down to the minutest detail, beginning with her clothes. She wore a khaki colored skirt, which went down to her ankles, naturally, and a denim blouse. Her *hijab* was made of a black fabric that had embroidered edges. Her shoes were chunky-heeled black boots and her jacket was her favorite multicolored block print of dark paisley flower patterns.

When the lumbering yellow whale, otherwise known as the school bus, arrived on her corner, she boarded it and took a seat near the front. Even though there were about fifteen other kids on the bus, everyone hushed when they saw her. Everyone knew what was going to happen after lunch.

Layla felt the stares like little pinpricks running up and down the back of her neck but she tried her best to ignore them. Little whispers from the back of the bus let her know she was the topic of everyone's gossip, at least for the moment. Getting nervous now certainly wouldn't help her.

As the bus driver worked to finish her route, Layla mused over all the different kinds of advice she had received so far. She still couldn't believe she hadn't told her parents anything at all about all of this. Even when she explained her detention and community service she had merely mentioned that a girl at school was picking on her and she was unjustly blamed. Her parents offered to intervene but Layla insisted that their help was not needed. Staying after school, she remarked, would be a great way to get a jump on her homework.

The noise in the bus steadily grew as the kids went back to other topics such as homework, teachers, TV shows and sports. An occasional paper ball flew out the window, someone would giggle over a stupid joke or two kids would start talking loudly about wrestling, a cool band or a new show.

Layla, however, didn't really notice any of it either way. It was then that she realized she had forgotten her lunch money. "Oh well," she thought, "fasting today wouldn't hurt."

"Oh, I'm so excited!" Michelle could hardly contain herself and she seemed to babble on and on about how she would steal the hearts and minds of the student body. That's how Layla felt about her banter, anyway, as she stood there, trapped by Michelle outside her fourth period classroom door.

"Oh, ah, Layla?" Michelle asked abruptly. "Do you have any idea what you're going to say?"

Layla shifted her weight onto her heels and replied, "Well, um, not really. I mean I have an idea but…"

Just then Michelle waved to someone she saw passing by in the hall. Turning back to Layla she blurted out hastily, "Hey, I gotta' go. Tell me about it later. That's Jimmy Sanger from the baseball team." She tilted her head and chirped, "If I'm seen with him for a while it'll make me look good. Every little bit helps. Bye."

Layla, who still felt that she was interrupted in mid-sentence, watched helplessly as her friend disappeared into the crowd. In the past she might have been more annoyed by Michelle's skittishness, but this time she let it pass. She had too much on her mind anyway.

After the next class would be lunch and after lunch came the student assembly. Everyone in the whole school would be there to listen to the candidates speak. She was a candidate. She would also have to give a speech.

Layla shook the unpleasant thought out of her head and stepped into her class just before the buzzer rang. She took her seat near the left wall and opened her book bag, echoing the actions of the other thirty or so students.

Ms. Wharton, who was also known among the students as "The Rake" on account of her neatly separated rows of hair, stood up from her seat and started writing on the board. "Take out your notebooks class and get ready to write," she bellowed. Layla obeyed mechanically while looking around the class for any sign that people were staring at her or whispering about her. She had no friends in this class but no open enemies, either, except for two girls that hung around Linda Patterson. But without their ringleader to guide them, they never really messed with her.

"Okay class," Ms. Wharton said, wearing a neat yellow blouse and dark blue skirt, "now take out your reading text and turn to page 147. We're going to begin reading an excerpt from Tom Sawyer. Who can tell me who wrote this story?"

The students were busy flipping the pages, looking in vain for the story so they could answer the question. Layla, who already knew the answer, raised her hand as the teacher scanned the room. "Yes, Layla. What is the answer?"

"Samuel Clemons, also known as Mark Twain."

"Good. Now let me give you a little background on this author." Ms. Wharton began writing on the board when a knock on the closed classroom door interrupted her. She put her chalk down and walked over to the door. The annoyance was clear on her face. If there's one thing every kid learns real fast, it's not to interrupt a teacher's train of thought, especially not an English teacher.

Ms. Wharton opened the door and scowled. There stood someone who was quite familiar to Layla, and most other students for that matter. It was Kelly Spitz, standing there in a torn, oversized shirt, a black knee-length leather skirt, chunky combat boots and that large silver necklace that hung too far down her neck. She was holding a note in her hand and she promptly handed it to the stunned teacher.

"What's this?" she asked.

"I've been kicked out of Mr. Brown's class. I guess they're moving me to your class." Kelly replied nonchalantly. Apparently she had done this thing before.

Not coincidentally, Kelly Spitz had a reputation among the teachers also. Ms. Wharton read and reread the note several times. A moment later she sighed and motioned with her hand to come inside. All the kids in the class stared at the new arrival as she walked defiantly into the room and took an empty seat near the back wall.

Layla was instantly disturbed by the new reality of her classroom. Kelly was a known troublemaker in any class she was in. Layla felt that the possibility of any future learning in this class was now DOA: Dead on Arrival.

Ms. Wharton resumed her lesson and gave several facts about Mark Twain before asking the class to read the opening section of the excerpt in their textbooks. Kelly, who had no book, was asked to share with the girl closest to her, but even though she moved her chair slightly, she showed no interest in the topic. She leaned back in her chair and chewed on a piece of gum, popping it loudly as if to emphasize an unspoken point.

After about five minutes, Ms. Wharton asked the class to summarize what they read in their notebooks. Everyone began writing as the teacher walked around the room, checking students' work here and there with her red pen. When she came to Kelly's desk she saw an open notebook filled with nothing but doodles.

"What's this?" She asked. "Didn't you read the excerpt? Write down what the opening section is about."

"I didn't get it." Kelly sneered.

The other students were pretending not to notice, but all ears were tuned to the trouble in the back of class. Ms. Wharton was known as a tough teacher and she had little time for lazy students. After a few more words exchanged, mostly whispered, Ms. Wharton said loudly, "I have just the solution. A peer tutor."

"I don't need no…" Kelly began protesting.

"I've made up my mind. Just grin and bear it. You'll be the better for it. Now, *who* will I choose?"

Layla felt a creeping feeling overcome her. She was one of the best students in class, she was not well liked by most of the students and she was known as a compliant girl who rarely complained.

"Layla!" The sound of the teacher's voice almost made an echo bounce out of her chest. But she knew she couldn't squirm out of it once the teacher made up her mind. *"Why Allah?"* she asked to herself, rolling her eyes upward. *"Why me?"*

Kelly, for her part, audibly groaned in displeasure as Ms. Wharton told Layla to move to the back of the room and take a seat near the new student in the class. Layla paused for a moment, sighed, and then gathered up her things and walked the four rows back to where Kelly sat.

As she passed by the other students, some of them smirked while a few looked sympathetic. Getting paired up with someone like Kelly Spitz was cruel and unusual punishment for anybody, even an unpopular girl like Layla. Kelly Spitz wasn't nice to *anybody*.

The class was mercifully short in Layla's estimation. Perhaps it was because her mind was truly elsewhere. Kelly squirmed and fidgeted in her seat as Layla explained patiently, though distractedly, how to do the in-class writing assignment. When the bell finally rang ending the period, Layla began to pack her book bag so she could get to the lunchroom as quickly as possible. She didn't want to speak to the student body about popularity, of course, but she also didn't want to compound her misery by showing up late.

As she stood up and prepared herself to join the throng of students rushing out into the hallway, Kelly made a loud popping sound with her chewing gum and said, "Go get 'em, Raggedy Anne."

Layla was taken by surprise and couldn't tell if it was a weird compliment or an insult. She had to go, though, so she just nodded slightly and left the room.

Lunch time. If there was ever a parallel with the great zoos of the world, the lunchroom in a junior high was it. Hungry students paced all around aimlessly like caged animals while others waited impatiently in lines that constantly seemed to change shape like a giant boa constrictor.

Food, and other objects that were not always identifiable, often found themselves flying through the air like bats, while loud catcalls and shouts pierced the general noisy din like the battle cries of feuding bulls.

Rumors of *mystery meat* and radioactive tater tots added fuel to the excitement of an already supercharged break for hoards of tired teenagers. *This crowd*, Layla thought to herself as she entered the large lunchroom and panned her eyes over the milling throngs, would be *her* audience.

The Student Council volunteers shouted ceaselessly, trying to get everyone seated properly. The students, all nine hundred of them, seemed to *want* to make life as difficult as possible for the organizers of the event, and the exasperation on the faces of the Council members showed it was working.

Layla walked through the maze of lunch tables and mused on the nature of the space before her. The large spacious cavern doubled as the auditorium and it seemed to be bursting with excitement, along with the occasional attendant flying food objects. Layla noted with satisfaction the hopelessness evident on some of the organizer's faces as they considered the fact that the rowdiness of lunchtime might carry over into the official assembly.

Layla approached the back of the room where there was an upraised stage which normally had a huge double curtain concealing the rear area during regular school days. The stage stretched from one end of the back of the lunchroom to the other and was really quite large. She ducked behind the left edge of the only partially opened curtain and stood off to the side where a few other students were standing.

As the student ushers and a few teachers were busy making sure that everyone was seated at the lunch tables, Layla peered out from behind the edge of the curtain and was thankful the audience was being made to discard any food or cans that were leftover from lunch. Visions of flying food directed right at her played over and over in her mind.

Mr. Gottbaum stood near the back of the partially hidden stage with a few teachers and talked over last minute schedule adjustments for the speeches. Layla, desperate to find any distraction to take her mind off the butterflies in her stomach, walked over to where her friend Michelle was standing. She was really starting to look excited and Layla quickly found out why.

"*This is it*!" she exclaimed, as the noise from outside the curtains began to die away. "Oh Layla, did you hear? Shelly MacPherson had to drop out. She got tonsillitis or something. What a lucky break! That's one less opponent; *aw, poor Shelly*. It's almost as if the *very stars* are on my side. I hope I do good. *Please God*," she implored, while looking upward, "let me win and become the most popular girl in school."

Layla mused for a moment over the worthiness of what her friend was asking God for and then said a humble prayer of her own. Rather than asking for the crowd to cheer her on, however, she asked God to help her get through it without messing up *too* badly.

Mr. Gottbaum walked over to Linda Patterson and was about to say some final instructions when he remembered something. He looked back over his shoulder and motioned to Layla and Michelle to come over to where he was standing. Shamika, who had been practicing her speech behind a table near the back right of the stage, was also called over.

"Now girls," he began, even before the other contestants were completely in his range of voice, "you only have five minutes to get your message across. If you go over the time you'll be asked to stop. Now, let's see, oh yeah, Linda will go first, then Michelle and then Shamika. Oh," he nodded in Layla's direction, "you'll go last."

Layla kind of figured that her turn would be in less than prime time. As the four girls made their way to the four lecterns placed on the stage, Layla began to hope that everyone would be bored by the time she was supposed to speak, that way she wouldn't have to worry about anyone getting out of hand or even remembering what she said later on.

As each of the girls moved behind her respective lectern, Layla peered nervously at the tall burgundy stage curtain that stood closed before her. In a moment it would part in two as it was drawn back, exposing a really hostile teenage audience. "*Qadr*," she mused, and then she whispered the words: "O Allah, help me to bear this burden." She then fixed her *hijab* and straightened her blouse.

Glancing sideways, she saw Michelle peering into a small pocket mirror. The next girl over was Linda Patterson. She looked confident and poised. Her perfectly styled sun-streaked brown hair and silk red blouse were quite a contrast with Michelle's white blouse and knee-length black skirt. At the furthest edge stood Shamika, who was wearing an expensive loose sweater with a sports logo and tight blue jeans. She had a blue sparkled hair clip holding her hair back in a wave.

Outside, the announcement was made that the candidates for the Most Popular Student contest were about to give their campaign speeches. The teenagers began clapping and whistling as the curtains were slowly withdrawn to either side of the stage.

Linda beamed with pleasure while Michelle waved profusely. Shamika smiled broadly and held her hands up in a sign of victory. Layla, however, simply stood there under the hot spotlights with a neutral expression on her face. She couldn't bring herself to smile or wave given that she didn't believe in what the contest was about. After all, she was only there to keep from getting an even *more* damaged reputation.

Mr. Gottbaum strode from behind the edge of the left curtain and took a wireless microphone out of his pocket. "Is this thing on?" He asked, fumbling with the "on" button.

Several laughs and catcalls from the crowds of students seated at the picnic style lunch tables told him it was.

"Welcome, students of Mansfield Junior High!" He announced excitedly.

The students erupted in cheers, not for Gottbaum mind you, but for their school which many took great pride in. It had a wonderful sports program and the football and baseball teams always won more games than they lost.

Mr. Gottbaum, though, thinking that he was the center of applause, grinned widely with his coffee stained teeth and raised his arm in the air for silence.

"Today, the candidates will speak to you on why they deserve your vote in the Most Popular Student contest. Each will be given five minutes to speak, no more. While they're talking, I expect everyone to be courteous and respectful. Do I make myself *clear*?"

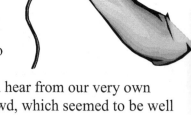

The students groaned in agreement in the halfhearted way that kids do when an adult tries to assert their authority over them.

"Good. Now first we will hear from our very own *Liiiindaaaa Patterson*." The crowd, which seemed to be well trained to support those who were already well-known, began cheering and clapping.

After Linda nodded and waved for a moment, with those perfect sparkling eyes and shiny teeth that made her popular already, Mr. Gottbaum motioned for silence and continued. "After that we will hear from Michelle Whitman, Shamika Thompkins and Layla Deen."

There was general but more muted applause, making Layla suspect that the results of the day were a foregone conclusion. Taking it all in stride, however, Michelle and Shamika did their best to look excited and wave back. Some of Shamika's supporters called out loudly, stood up, whistled and raised their arms in the arm triumphantly.

Layla noticed for the first time just how much this contest meant to Michelle and Shamika, not because they so desperately needed to be popular, but because, it seemed more and more apparent to Layla, that they were jealous of *Linda's* popularity.

They saw in her someone they wished they could be. It was tempting, Layla mused, as she watched the vice principal walk to the side of the stage, to want to be known everywhere you go, to have doors held open and people inviting you to all the best parties. But Layla was mindful of her stark vision in the bathroom mirror before. She firmly believed now that quietly doing the best you can without worrying *who* thought *what* about you *was* the way a truly confident person should be.

When Mr. Gottbaum called for Linda to speak, she smiled at the cheering students and began by saying, "My fellow students, every school needs to be represented by the best and brightest it has to offer. Skill in dealing with all sorts of situations requires brains, as well as *beauty*." At that several jocks in the front row called out and cheered.

Linda smiled demurely and continued, saying, "Through my high grades and already well-known social strength, I believe I am the most logical choice. I'm already one of the most popular students in this school's history and my parties are where all the movers and shakers go. Therefore, I'm the natural leader."

Layla profoundly wished that she was anywhere else but here, listening to the gushing praise this girl was heaping upon herself. Linda continued talking about her 'achievements' of the last several years: the medals in cheerleading, the food drives, the student council work she's done, and then she wowed the crowd with a rousing tribute to all the popular girls who attended the school in years past.

She wound down her speech by saying, "So in conclusion, I want to say that I love you all and that I know you'll make the right choice and pick the girl who is already unofficially the most popular girl anyway. When I'm chosen for this honor I'll go on being the best and the brightest so you can be proud that you go to Mansfield Junior High! Thank you all and goodbye."

The students clapped and cheered excitedly, while a few obnoxious boys booed for fun. To add to the din, some of Linda's friends were obviously trying to keep the clapping going when Mr. Gottbaum came out on stage and called again for silence.

After the hooting and catcalling had died away, Mr. Gottbaum introduced Michelle and invited the crowd to hear her address with the same respect as they showed to Linda Patterson. For her part, when her name was announced again, Michelle smiled so broadly and stood so erect that Layla thought she had a board stuck to her back.

The students cheered, though not as intensely as before, and Michelle began to speak. "My friends," she began. "As you know, every school reaches a point in its existence when it must examine itself and decide where it wants to go. Will the school get stuck in the past," and when she said those words she nodded firmly in Linda's direction, much to the amusement of the audience. Linda, however, showed by her frown that she was clearly not amused.

"Or," Michelle continued, when the snickers died down, "will the school look to the future." When she said that last word she tilted her head to the side, smiled and bobbed once for emphasis while spreading her hands up in the air.

Layla listened and was quite entertained by Michelle's veiled attacks on the "old order" of the usual popular crowd and how a breath of fresh air could really energize a school and propel it ever higher and farther.

Then Michelle spoke of a litany of good causes the school should support from saving endangered species to stopping global warming. All of this caused Layla to have a newfound respect for her erstwhile friend and she put her fascination in her mental in-box of: "Wow, I never knew that about her" things. A few minutes later Michelle was ready to bring her speech to a close.

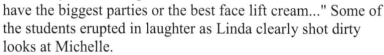

"So in conclusion," she said while smiling broadly, "I would like to say that although I don't have the biggest parties or the best face lift cream..." Some of the students erupted in laughter as Linda clearly shot dirty looks at Michelle.

"I do have a genuine and honest personality and I can still dress to kill with the best of them. Vote for me and get a fresh new face to represent Mansfield Junior High!"

The crowd now applauded much stronger for Michelle than they had before. Even Layla, herself, had to admit that it was a pretty good speech with certainly a much more relevant message for the students than Linda's exercise in self-glorification.

Next up was Shamika. She looked a little nervous when Gottbaum announced her turn to explain to the students why they should support her. The applause was respectable and Shamika seemed emboldened by some of the loud calls of her friends, "You go girl!" "That's right, more ice to the nice!"

Shamika stood up straighter and began her speech by saying, "Students of Mansfield Junior High, my name is Shamika Thompkins. I've been a student here for two years. I've seen a lot of stuff and been around. It seems to me the most popular student in school should represent the best in our school, not the worst. There's so many cliques and groups and all. Seems somebody is always puttin' somebody else down. We are better than that."

The crowd listened more reflectively and seemed stunned by the radical change in tone. Shamika spoke of how a student representative should be a symbol of unity and that the most popular student had a special duty to unify all students so everyone can share in the best the school environment has to offer. Layla was also moved by the impassioned plea and felt a little less nervous.

"And so I say in conclusion," Shamika intoned at the end of her allotted time, "that it's not just about being popular that counts, but being real. Being real to everybody so nobody thinks they're better than anybody else. Thank you and goodbye."

When Shamika spoke her final words the students again erupted in bigger and louder cheers than they gave Linda. The first speaker simply smiled politely at her chief rival and then scanned the audience for her friends, hoping they would yell 'booooo.' They didn't seem to be doing much of anything, much to Linda's chagrin. "I'll fix them later." Linda thought to herself.

Gottbaum walked over on the stage to quiet the crowd down. "All right. All Right. Now we have our last speaker," he nodded his head over to Layla. "It's Layla Deen."

The students, still excited from Shamika's rousing rendition, clapped more heartily than Layla expected. She felt oddly elated and much of her nervousness left her. Remembering what she had learned in Sunday School a long time before, Layla began by saying, "Greetings, my fellow students. My name is Layla Deen. Perhaps some of you know me, but most of you, I think, don't. I've never tried to make waves since entering junior high. I never wanted to be popular. I've only tried to be just myself."

As she began her speech and the honesty of her words became apparent to the audience; the last vestiges of whispering left the crowd. "I have always tried to be respectful to everyone I met. I have not always been respected by others. What has been the case, in fact, is that I have often been disrespected by other students simply because of my style of dress. Maybe there are other reasons but I don't know them."

Layla suddenly began to feel as if it were her right to tell everyone how she's been feeling for over a year. Her soul seemed to open and her fears began to melt away as the full force of her emotion took over.

"My religion is different from what many of you follow. I am a Muslim, and I have teachings and beliefs I hold dear. I never thought that my way of praying to God or the way my religion asks me to dress would make people hate me, but sometimes it seems to me that that's the case. I've never insulted anyone else about their beliefs or clothes and I believe it is wrong for people to do that to me."

The students sat silently and even the teachers seemed to listen more carefully to this soul searching plea. As Layla scanned the crowd she picked out faces that were familiar to her. There was Mandy and Lisa, Matthew and Jim, kids who had been in the same elementary school as her who now didn't know her from a hole in the wall.

Then she saw Aishah and Sultana, two of her Muslim classmates who tried their best to blend in and avoid her. These were the people who had changed. She didn't. She was the same Layla, honest, outgoing and friendly, yet forced into the box of isolation by people who judged her too harshly for petty reasons.

Layla shifted her weight to a more even stance and continued, "My religion asks the question: 'Is is right to judge others because they are a little different?' Do we shun people who are not like us, who don't wear the most expensive clothes or go to the right parties or want boyfriends? Is it right to

81

idolize the popular and vilify the quiet, the misunderstood or the different?" Layla saw Kelly Spitz's face in the crowd, looking as mesmerized as the rest.

"The Prophet of my religion taught that people should not be judged by their looks or their bodies. He said you should only judge people by what's in their hearts and minds. This noble idea found its way into modern times when Dr. Martin Luther King said that his dream was for people to be judged by the content of their character and not by the color of their skin." Several of the students, Shamika's friends among them, nodded and said, "That's right." "Speak on, girl."

"I am not deserving of the most popular award. I'm not even popular." Layla smirked on that last remark. "I didn't even want to enter this contest. As long as I am here I want the real story to be told. Popularity can be a curse and not a blessing if a person takes their lofty position as a sign that they're better than others. I believe the most popular person should be the one who serves others before themselves, who helps those who are in need and who tells everyone around them things that will elevate their spirits and not just feed their whims."

Quite without Layla's planning, the students began to nod their heads and look on approvingly, a smile here, a glance there, so much so that Layla let any lingering fear disappear.

"My fellow students," Layla continued, "I am not here to ask for your vote today. I don't want to be voted into popularity. All I ask is that you pay more attention to the feelings of others and not judge them by what they wear, how they look or what they believe. We are all part of the same human family and the best person is the one who is the best in their heart. If everyone is always concerned with who is the best looking, the richest or the coolest then we're focusing on the wrong things in our lives. What about the kids who have nothing or the ill who only want to be cured? Who will ask about them or care about what they're going through? If being popular means you are the center of attention then the attention of the people is in the wrong place."

Layla was as surprised by her eloquence and persuasive arguments as the students and even the teachers were. Everyone was completely silent now. Linda, Shamika and Michelle were also looking on intently.

Layla nodded towards the students nearest to her and said, "I hope that when you are making your choice for who is most popular that you choose not on the basis of looks, money or reputation, but for the one who is the best person inside and the kindest to others. I'm not saying that's me, because I've pretty much kept to myself since entering this school, but there must be one of these three," Layla raised her arm and gestured towards her stunned opponents, "who has the potential to do more good with your vote than harm. Choose wisely and remember that popularity should be determined by service to others, not by how much service one can get for herself. Thank you all for listening."

There was a moment of silence after her last words that made Layla feel as if she were going to be jeered and booed at any moment. It was Shamika who broke the silence by a single clap of her hands, a pause then another clap. Almost as if on cue the audience began clapping in a rhythmic fashion nearly as one. After a brief moment a general burst of applause erupted and many students got to their feet and cheered and waved.

Layla was not expecting this outpouring of support and blushed. Michelle walked over and hugged her friend and whispered, "That was the best speech I ever heard. You're *so right*."

Mr. Gottbaum waltzed out on the stage, acting once more as if the applause was for him, smiling and waving. He took the microphone and raised his hand for silence. "There you have it," he began, talking loudly to force a cessation of the noise.

"These are your candidates. Now we ask you to observe them in action over the next two weeks. This is your time to scrutinize their behavior, activities and qualifications for this honor. At the end of the two weeks, ballots will be coming around during your seventh period classes and you will have to make your choice proclaiming the most popular student in the school. The results will then be announced a week after that at our school's annual homecoming game."

At the mention of the big game the students erupted in cheers. Mr. Gottbaum struggled to make his voice heard over the roar of the crowd and managed to say only, "Thank you for your cooperation and think about what you've heard with an open and clear mind. Now back to your regularly scheduled classes"

Layla watched as the vice-principal called erratically on the teachers to help in the chaotic dismissal. Her view of the mayhem was cut short by the closing of the curtain in front of her, leaving her and her fellow candidates in a kind of ruddy red-flavored dimness.

Michelle and Shamika both came to congratulate Layla and she complimented them back. Linda walked over a moment later and sneered, "What a goody two shoes speech, *Lula*. I hope you don't join the Peace Corps too soon or you'll miss my victory parade at the homecoming game next month."

Shamika exclaimed, "Hey, lay off Deen. She's alright."

Linda swished her hair as she turned to go and grumbled something inaudibly as she slipped out of the left side of the stage in search of her supporters.

Michelle chattered on for the next ten minutes about her speech and about how she hoped it would sway the students. Layla thought she heard her say something to the effect that she was glad that she, Layla, told people not to vote for her, otherwise they would choose based on the best speech alone.

Layla took her leave the first chance she got and entered the hallway to go back to class. The other students were long back in their seats and Layla wondered how she would make it through the rest of the day.

12

Two weeks had passed and life returned to normal for Layla. In fact, it was better than normal on several fronts. Although no one rushed forward to be her friend, at least she received a few more friendly glances than before. She felt better about herself, as well, which seemed to her like someone lifted a heavy stone off her back. For that she felt the experience was priceless.

The balloting had gone smoothly the day before and even though the Student Council members were a big part of the entire process, the results of the popularity contest were being kept a secret by the guidance counselors and in any event, they would not be announced until the halftime show at the upcoming homecoming football game.

Layla was finished with her detention sentence and completed the last of her CPR classes just two days before. It wasn't actually that bad, she told herself, and she felt proud that she now knew such an important skill. It had been an easier (and shorter) class than she had expected and although it was pretty weird to do mouth-to-mouth on a life-sized rubber dummy, she passed the course with a good grade and got a certificate to boot.

The thought crossed her mind afterwards that she might like to sign up for another student volunteer class to broaden her horizons even further, but that would have to wait until her mind was a bit clearer. As she dressed herself for the long school day ahead of her, a lingering thought hung in her mind: how would she survive attending a junior high football game? All the candidates were required to be there to hear the results, and she had never gone to such an event in her life. She smirked wryly and imagined how it might be.

Soon she was ready to leave for school. As she hoisted her book bag over her shoulder and made her way out of the house towards the bus stop, though, a new and very alarming thought occurred to her. Layla wasn't worried about losing the contest and being embarrassed by it publicly. Not at all, in fact.

She had been telling everybody she knew that she didn't want to win. After the Friday speeches two weeks before she couldn't imagine making the point any clearer. But it suddenly occurred to her that after that unintentionally brilliant speech she gave about the meaninglessness of popularity, that if she *did* win, by some fluke - a really big fluke - it would be really uncomfortable for her.

She talked about that possibility during Sunday school with Rayhanna who also raised the strange prospect that the most *unpopular* girl might win after an unprecedented upset. In any case, Rayhanna said cheerfully, the results will be announced soon, and then it would all be over for Layla. This is, of course, what Layla also tried to focus on.

Layla passed that Monday in a daze and scarcely paid attention in any of her classes. She just couldn't take her focus off the contest and how she wouldn't be able to relax until it was all behind her. There was one class, however, where she distinctly had to be on her guard and had to put aside all worries of anything else: English.

She was still assigned to be Kelly Spitz's tutor, a job that was more of a punishment from a vindictive teacher than a good deed. After a couple of days of resistance, though, Kelly actually was a bit calmer. Layla's patience and non-judgmental attitude seemed to put her at ease.

On this particular day, Kelly seemed apprehensive. The teacher had given the class a group work assignment requiring each pair of students to identify the plot in a lyric poem and how each character fits in. Over the low drone of students whispering to each other, Layla tried her best to get Kelly to participate. She just sat there, though, staring into the distance as if she could see something far away that no one else could.

Layla, of course, could have done the assignment perfectly well on her own but she had grown used to Kelly noisily sitting near her and felt strange at her sudden quietness. Unable to stand it any longer, Layla put down her pen and paper and whispered, "Hey, Kelly, you feeling okay?"

Kelly merely looked down and said, "Yeah, I'm, ah... okay." She had become used to Layla, as well and seemed to an odd sort of ease around her. With Layla she realized that she didn't have to put up a front. "Well, I wanted to tell you something but..." she let her words trail off.

"But what? You can tell me." Layla implored.

Just then Kelly's notebook slipped off the desk and fell to the floor with a loud thud. All eyes turned to the pair who had disturbed the otherwise harmonious work atmosphere that had blanketed the class. Ms. Wharton looked up and rolled her eyes menacingly. Kelly bent down to pick up her book and part of her arm above the wrist became exposed out of her sleeve. Layla saw it and Kelly suddenly realized she had been careless. There on Kelly's forearm was a large welt. It looked fresh and had already turned many colors as it attempted to heal. She quickly jerked her arm back up and into her long sleeve and looked away. Layla sat stunned.

She was no fool, though, and she knew when it was better to pretend that nothing was seen or heard. But she couldn't help but feel an immediate concern for her obviously troubled peer. It was not that Layla considered Kelly a friend, but rather she had always had a streak of compassion in her for the downtrodden that ran extremely strong.

She remembered the time when she and her brother, Ahmad, tracked down a poor man who had stolen from their home. While she was angry at first, after they discovered that the homeless man had only stolen food to feed some abandoned kittens she resolved never to be so judgmental of others again. Real people's lives, she learned to recognize, were far deeper and more complicated than she could ever understand.

For the rest of the class, Layla paid more attention to Kelly and told her more than once that if there was any other help she could give her that she shouldn't hesitate to ask.

When the period ended, Layla began to pack her book bag when suddenly Kelly spoke up, saying, "Hey Deen," her tone of voice was softer than usual, "can we, I, um you know, can we *talk*?"

Layla paused for a moment. Kelly had never asked her for anything before. "Uh, sure," she said as coolly as possible. "Next period is lunch. We can go to the cafeteria together." Kelly silently picked up her own book bag, shoved her ratty notebook in it and followed Layla out of the class.

It was a strange walk to the cafeteria for Layla. She was being followed closely by the most notorious girl in school. She didn't walk besides her; rather Kelly trailed along like an ominous shadow. Layla wondered what she could possibly want with her, and what about that nasty bruise?

A few moments later, the pair entered the lunchroom and Layla slowed down so Kelly could catch up and walk beside her. Ignoring the few stares she was receiving, most probably on account of the company she was keeping that day, Layla steered Kelly to a lonely table in the rear corner that was Layla's usual refuge during lunchtime.

Both girls sat down, across from each other, in silence. Layla looked at Kelly, who kept her head in a downward pose and asked her, "So you want something to eat?" Kelly didn't say a word, but Layla could tell she was not exactly a model for good nutrition.

Since the bulk of the students had not yet entered the lunchroom, Layla realized that if she were quick enough she could get through the food line before it really filled up. She told Kelly she would be right back and then scurried towards the line, which at that time had only about a dozen or so students ahead of her.

As she moved closer to the serving station, Layla surveyed the food offerings behind the glass and chrome display tables. After a passing thought wafted through her mind about the mysterious lives of the cafeteria workers, Layla indicated her choices to the lunch lady behind the counter.

In short order, a plate of mashed potatoes, a smaller plate of green beans and a jello cup were handed over the top and placed on Layla's grey plastic tray. After paying the cashier two dollars, Layla purposefully wound her way through the zigzagging students back to where Kelly was waiting for her.

As she got closer to the table, however, Layla noticed that it was glaringly empty. Kelly was nowhere to be seen. "Great," Layla thought to herself as she sat down and stared at the impossibly vacant seat in front of her. After a moment's pause, she picked up her plastic spoon and began fidgeting in the potatoes, drawing lines and making artificial craters.

She thought that Kelly might have gone to the bathroom and would return momentarily, but ten minutes passed with no sign of her returning. "Oh well," Layla thought to herself, as she began to eat. "Maybe I'll see her later in the hall."

But Layla, try as she might, couldn't concentrate on the food before her, and not just because it didn't taste particularly well. She felt a nagging sensation that seemed to tug her away. Kelly had a really bad bruise and she had asked to talk.

Layla's inner sense of compassion was kindled and showed no signs of abating.

After a few more bites of the pasty potatoes, Layla could ignore that feeling no longer. She took her tray to the trash can, emptied it and laid it on top of the receptacle. Then she left the lunchroom in search of Kelly.

A search of the bathroom turned up nothing. Ditto for the gym. There was still about half an hour left of lunch period so Layla surmised she would have time to complete her quest, but after another fruitless ten minutes of wandering the halls, Layla was about to give up. Then a flicker of inspiration flashed in her mind.

With a renewed sense of purpose, Layla set off back to the gym. She entered and ignored the stares of the students who had gathered there after lunch to play basketball and socialize. Then she walked into the locker room and began her search. Kelly wasn't in the shower area or in one of the stalls, but Layla was not discouraged.

She approached the back exit door, the one that led out onto the soccer field, and carefully opened it. Students were not supposed to use that door but in cases of emergency, and Layla could get in trouble if she were caught, but by this time she had invested too much time in her search top worry about that now.

Warm air and the fresh smell of sunshine-baked grass wafted over her senses, and then she instantly understood the allure of skipping classes to get some "outside time." Careful to hold the door so it wouldn't close behind her, Layla stepped outside and looked around.

After scanning the soccer field in the distance, Layla noticed the unmistakable figure of Kelly Spitz sitting on an aluminum bench just off to the side of the spectator stands. Steeling herself for what she was about to do, Layla picked up a nearby stone and used it to prop the door slightly open. Then she slowly walked towards the enigmatic object of her search.

Kelly looked up in surprise when she saw Layla approaching. "What'r you doin' here? Don't you know you could get in trouble?" Kelly asked, with a hint of sincerity to her voice.

Layla said nothing and sat down beside her. She could see that Kelly had been crying. "What's wrong?" she asked, while shifting to turn closer.

Kelly momentarily stiffened her back, as if to shout, "Nothing!" but instead she slumped forward and put her elbows on her knees. "I got beat last night," she muttered matter-of-factly. "I don't know what I did wrong."

As if to emphasize the point, Kelly lifted her right sleeve, revealing more than one nasty looking bruise. One of them looked faintly like the outline of a hand print, as if someone was holding the arm so hard it seared their marks into Kelly's flesh.

Layla was shocked for a moment, but then leaned closer to Kelly and tentatively put her arm around her shoulder. Kelly instantly responded to the kind gesture and all but melted into Layla's embrace. She then started to cry, lightly at first but then with ever increasing sorrow.

Layla held Kelly close and let her cry as long as she wanted. She resolved not to let heaven or earth move her from her spot until Kelly got it all out. Kelly's tears caused Layla to have a momentary flashback. It reminded Layla of the time she found her mother crying over her relatives and how they ostracized her. Layla had hugged her mother then and let her cry, though she didn't know how to make it better. She understood that sometimes there is no better, and that you just have to let the crying happen until there's no more tears to fall. Kelly would get that and more, Layla thought to herself.

Another twenty minutes passed of Layla just holding Kelly in a frozen embrace. She knew lunchtime was over, and that she was missing her next class, but somehow those concerns took on less urgency than even Layla expected.

After a few more minutes of stillness, Kelly began to unravel her tale of woe. She explained how her mother's boyfriend was a drunk, and how he used to beat her mother. Then she darkly whispered that recently the man had been pushing her around and bullying her.

Layla listened in rapt attention, without saying a word, as Kelly recounted her descent into substance abuse as a way to cope with the constant stress and pain of her home life. All that she was hearing was so different from her own experience, it almost made Layla feel embarrassed for having such an otherwise safe and predictable lifestyle.

Kelly then described the beating she got the night before. Layla was distraught at the vivid recounting she was privy to, and she tried her best to understand the level of violence that was depicted. Kelly then pointed out each bruise on her arm and explained how each was received.

"You should tell one of the guidance counselors about this," Layla offered, by way of suggestion.

"Naah," Kelly responded. "They all think I'm nuts and the first thing they'd do is call my house and then would I ever get it then."

"There must be something we can do about this. You can't go back to that house, not now."

"I got nowhere else to go, and besides I get in enough trouble as is. I know how to survive."

Layla focused in on Kelly's face as she spoke. She had that edge of sadness that comes with troubled girls; an edge that no amount of heavy eye-liner and rouge could cover up. Layla wanted so desperately to help, but beyond asking for the aid of adults, she couldn't think of anything else.

"Don't tell nobody 'bout this. Promise?"

The abruptness of Kelly's request startled Layla, but unable to think of any other course of action, she answered meekly by saying, "Okay." Then she added, "But if you need someone to talk to, I'm here for you."

Kelly smiled gratefully in that half-broken way that people do when they're hurting inside, and then she stood up and walked away, though not I the direction of the school building.

Layla sat motionless and watched her go. A slight breeze welled up from somewhere and the cool edges of its touch softly swirled about her face as she realized she should go, too.

She rose to her feet, pausing once again to look at the receding figure of Kelly Spitz in the distance, and then she made her way back to the emergency door that led back into the locker room.

As luck would have it, the stone was still lodged in the door jamb, affording Layla the opportunity to slip back in the school unnoticed. When she reentered the main hall that led away from the gym, she heard the bell ring, ending the previous class period.

Layla was relieved when she realized that she could go to her next class without incident, but she silently prayed that her absence from the previous period would go unnoticed. For the rest of the day, she would be lost in thought, and into the night, as well.

13

"*Assalamu 'alaykum*, Rayhanna. It's Layla. I just wanted to say how happy I am for you that Fatimah got married. I heard it was an awesome wedding. Well, give me a call sometime. *Assalamu 'alaykum*."

Layla hung up the phone and sat still for a moment on the edge of her bed. She really wished she could have gone to Fatimah's wedding, but her parents didn't really know Rayhanna's parents so they weren't invited.

Layla thought about the last wedding her family had gone to. It was a really fancy one at one of those big hotel ballrooms. That was last year and it seemed like forever for her because dressing up was one of her favorite activities, and it had been a while since she had the opportunity to do that.

"Hmmm," thought Layla. "How ironic then that I have to dress up for Saturday's homecoming game."

The big football game was coming up and she who had never had any interest in going to one before was now being forced to go to hear the results of the Popularity Contest. "I don't even want to go," Layla blurted out involuntarily.

"Go where?" a curious little voice inquired. Layla looked at the door to her room and it was slightly ajar. A little face was peering in the crack held open by a set of little fingers on the door.

"That's none of your business, Hafsa," Layla said, allowing a slight tone of annoyance to enter her voice.

Not getting the hint, Hafsa flung open the door and bounced into the room as only little kids can do. "Layla's gonna' be popular. Layla's gonna' be popular," Hafsa chanted, as she ran around in a tight circle on Layla's oval throw rug.

Layla picked up a pillow and threw
away, short stuff. I've got problems of my

Hafsa picked up the pillow and thre
hitting her on the shoulder. Then she giggl
room and down the stairs.

Layla got up and closed her door; t
over to her bed and flopped stomach-first c
mattress. She grabbed a pillow and pushed __ _____ ___ ____
as she contemplated the week's unfolding events.

On Monday she had that strange meeting with Kelly
Spitz at the soccer field. Although she thought Kelly might
seek her out again after that, except for seeing her in English
class, Kelly made no mention of anything new and otherwise
ignored her.

On Tuesday Linda Patterson saw her in the crowded
hallway and called her a raghead in front of everyone. Layla
just ignored it at the time, but she couldn't help but wonder
why Linda hated her so.

Wednesday was normal but Thursday, from which she
had just gotten home, was horrific in terms of the amount of
homework the teachers assigned. That day she had come home
with an extremely overloaded book bag, and on the bus ride
home one of her straps broke, forcing her to carry the bundle in
her arms. As she lay on her bed, the ache in her muscles was
still fresh – and sore to boot!

Looking over at her desk, with its endless seeming pile
of books, Layla hoped she wouldn't be up too late. She had to
decide what she would wear to the game on Saturday, and she
instinctively knew that her cultural garb from her father's side
of the family was most probably not an option. This would
take some thought indeed.

Layla considered her time options. If she couldn't put
an outfit together that night, there was still Friday. She just
hoped that nothing crazy would happen on that day, as well.

ous feelings began to well
her. What happens at junior
ootball games? How do people
ss? What was she supposed to do
here? She had been to some track meets
to watch her brother Ahmad in the past,
but they were always held in the day,
and she was always sitting with one
parent or another.

Although Ahmad would be able to drop her off on
Saturday night as the school sports field, he couldn't stay due
to other commitments. Her parents also were busy. Hafsa had
a little kid party to go to with her mother and her father would
be at some community meeting in the *Masjid*.

Layla was more than a little hoping that her parents
would forbid her from going alone to the school homecoming
game, but in this case they said she was old enough and could
attend. Ahmed would drop her off and pick her up at set times.

Layla rolled over on her back and stared at her cream
colored ceiling. She began to imagine all sorts of scenarios for
Saturday. Linda Patterson would be announced the winner at
half-time. She would look so stunning and would rise like a
princess in the sky to give her acceptance speech. The first
thing she would do is point to Layla and laugh. The crowds
would laugh along with her and Layla would shrink to the size
of an ant and scurry away in some dark hole.

Then the image shifted in Layla's mind. Michelle
would be the one who was crowned the Most Popular. She
would be so excited that she would dissolve into a glittering
bubble of sparkles. Each sparkle would suddenly erupt in
chatter about how lucky she was and all at once they would
swirl around Layla's head, jabbering away until Layla's head
exploded from the ceaseless blabbering.

The sound of Ahmad shooting hoops outside her
window brought Layla back to earth. She felt an otherwise

stillness in her room and contemplated her homework once more. Slowly, she forced her limbs to pick her up off the bed and she sauntered unwillingly over to her desk. As she sat down and prepared to tackle her English homework, Layla wondered what the next day would hold for her.

She heard her door creak open, ever so slowly, and instinctively reached over for a pillow to throw. Hafsa was trying to sneak up on her, but this time she would be the first to get a hit. At least that momentary distraction brought a smile to Layla's face.

14

Friday came and with it a sense of foreboding. The mood of the students in the school was a mixture of quiet anticipation and exuberant chaos. Everyone had a different reason to feel excited.

The jocks were pumped over the upcoming game. They would be facing a team from another town that they had beaten last year. They were certain they would do so again and it showed in their swaggering through the halls. It seemed to Layla that every other boy had some type of sports shirt with big numbers on it. She had heard from Ahmad that high school jocks were worse, but at this moment, watching a trio of jocks pushing their way through the crowded hall yelling, Layla could not imagine how it could get worse than this.

Of course, much of the rest of the student body was excited for its own reasons. The Pep Squad had done its job in heightening the general level of excitement, and the cheerleaders were complicit it this, as well.

Although it was only going on third period, Layla noticed the frustration in the teachers' faces at how rowdy their classes were thus far. A few people had even pointed her out in the hallways and said positive things like, "Hey Deen! Good luck tomorrow," and "Yo Deen! Wat up?" Since she wasn't used to strangers calling her out in public, she couldn't decide if it were a good thing or a bad thing.

But the greatest undercurrent of excitement was from the girls. The results of the Popularity Contest were to be announced, and the female population of the school had really divided into three camps reflecting their favored choices.

The snooty girls all backed Linda Patterson. The tough athletic girls supported Shamika Thompkins, while the middle-of-the-road girls placed an inordinate amount of hope in the person of Michelle Whitman. Layla had already seen arguments break out among the supporters of each faction and she was extremely glad that she could squeak by unnoticed through the throngs of highly energized girls.

Third period came and went and fourth period was about to begin. That meant Ms. Wharton and her peculiar ways. She was very strict and it would be unlikely for the students to act rowdy in her class. Layla sighed in relief as she sat down in her usual seat. She hated classes full of disruptive students and the first three periods had been full of them.

When class time commenced, Ms. Wharton closed the door and began asking students to take out their homework from the night before. Layla opened her folder to get hers out when the thought struck her, Kelly was not in class. It wasn't all that unusual for her to be absent from school, but she had been in class everyday this week thus far.

Layla handed her homework forward to the girl in front of her and then sat back in her chair. The new knowledge she had about Kelly and her situation made her worried, and she made a mental note to look for her at lunchtime.

The bell rang signaling the end of fourth period. Layla was already packed and ready to leave the room and rushed past an astonished Ms. Wharton without a word. Because she was able to leave the class immediately, Layla had a clear path for at least half a minute or more.

She double-stepped to the lunchroom and scanned it as quickly as she could. No Kelly. From there to the locker room was only one main hallway, so if she kept her eyes open she would notice it if Kelly were anywhere to be found along the way.

With that thought in mind, Layla walked purposefully towards the gymnasium, artfully dodging the ever-growing clusters of students along the way. When she finally made it to the gym, she saw a handful of cheerleaders inside, practicing their routines for Saturday's game.

Layla ignored them and headed straight for the locker room. Upon entering, she paused to listen but heard nothing save for the bubbly chatter of a few cheerleaders in the sink area around the corner. She surmised that Kelly must be outside, so she made her way to the emergency exit door, opened it, stepped outside, propped it ajar with the same stone she had used before and began to walk towards the soccer field.

She reached the silver, aluminum bench where she had spoken with Kelly before, but it was empty. Kelly was nowhere to be found. Layla turned in a slow circle, scanning every direction, but still no sign of the object of her search.

After a few minutes pause, Layla turned to go back to the school. She wondered what Kelly was doing. Was she in school at all or somewhere on a deserted street, scared and alone? Layla remembered her heartfelt crying – the pain, the raw emotions and the sense of helplessness that permeated that fateful encounter.

Her musings were interrupted, however, as she approached the door that led back into the school. As she reached for the handle to open it, she was suddenly startled by a piercing scream. It was coming from within the building.

Layla opened the door and rushed inside. She heard a gaggle of alarmed voices coming from the shower area. She quick-stepped around the corner leading into that part of the locker room and found a crowd of about seven cheerleaders in the corner.

One of them was crouching down, holding what looked like a person in her arms. Layla rushed forward and saw that it was Kelly Spitz on the ground. The Cheerleader, a girl named Roseanne, looked panicked, even as the standing girls shook nervously and all talked over each other.

"What happened?" Layla cried out, as she pushed her way through two of the cheerleaders and kneeled down by Kelly.

"I don't know," Roseanne nervously yelped. "We were coming in to fix our hair when we heard a loud moaning sound and heard a thump in here."

"When we came in," one of the standing girls added, "we saw Kelly shaking on the floor. Then she just went still. It happened so fast."

"What do we do?" another girl cried out in a panic. Layla noticed it was Linda Patterson.

Layla looked at all the girls standing there and said, "One of you go get help. Go to the office!"

The girls looked at each other in frozen stares, so Layla pointed to Linda in particular and said, "You go! Now!"

Linda turned and ran out of the locker room, screaming for help.

Layla then looked at Kelly. She was indeed still.

"What do we do," Roseanne said, pleading to no one in particular.

Layla then had an instantaneous flashback. She suddenly remembered what she learned in her CPR class. "In an emergency," her instructor said, "do the ABC's." Layla immediately recounted the meaning of each: Check Airways, Breathing and Circulation.

She said to the girls around her, "I know what to do. Help me lay her flat."

Roseanne and two other girls carefully helped Layla to lay Kelly on her back. Layla opened Kelly's mouth and proceeded to swirl her finger inside. There was no obvious obstruction. Then she put her hand just over Kelly's lips and nose to detect breathing. Nothing. Then she grabbed her wrist to feel for a pulse. Again, nothing.

"Begin CPR," Layla intoned, following the instructions of what her teacher taught her to say in such situations.

Layla then bent over Kelly's face, pinched her nose and then blew a long breath into Kelly's mouth. Abruptly she sat up, put her two hands together in a combined fist and pumped up and down on Kelly's chest, right where her heart was located.

She then repeated the breathing, followed by the pumping for another full minute. "Is she gonna' be alright?" one of the girls asked. "Shhhhsh," Roseanne said. "Let Layla do her thing. I know what she's doing."

A moment later there was a coughing sound. Kelly heaved and her lifeless body seemed to come back to life. She grimaced and Layla twisted around to support her head as she coughed a few more times. Roseanne also moved closer to help support Kelly's shoulders.

Layla cradled Kelly's head in her arms. Kelly opened her eyes and looked up at the faces hovering before her. One face in particular, however, stood out for her and not solely because of its closer proximity.

"La.. Layla?" Kelly asked in a stupefied voice.

"Shhh," Layla answered, moving one had up to stroke Kelly's hair. "It's all right now."

The sound of shouting and the thump of many people pouring into the gym signaled the arrival of help. A moment later Layla found herself pushed to the side as school staff rushed into the shower area of the locker room. The last thing she saw before being herded out of the room with the other students was Kelly looking in her direction, her eyes seemed to be saying, "Thank you."

15

The confusion of the day passed by in a blur for Layla, even as it did for much of the student body. After being pushed out of the locker room along with the cheerleaders who had found Kelly Spitz unresponsive and not breathing, Layla ambled off down the hallway leading to the lunchroom.

The sound of an ambulance pulling up to the front of the school caused a major distraction, and the students who were enjoying the last few minutes of lunch period came out from every corner to watch what was happening. The bell signaling the start of fifth period rang, but for the most part the students and many staff members ignored it.

About twenty minutes later paramedics carried Kelly out on a rolling gurney. She had an oxygen mask over her face and her eyes were closed. When the ambulance finally drove away, school administrators and teachers tried to restore order.

"Back to class!" "Go to your fifth period class!" they barked incessantly.

Layla followed the shell shocked students as they made their ways to their next classes. A steadily rising din of discussion, questions and other related chatter arose as the hallways slowly emptied. There wouldn't be anything going on in anyone's fifth period that day.

Layla kept to herself, as always, and the absence of seeing Michelle for the remainder of the day was a blessing in her estimation. She didn't want any mindless blithering from her or anyone else. She hoped that Kelly would be all right.

Layla passed through sixth period uneventfully, as well. She heard the students whispering and chatting with each other. It seemed to her that at about halfway through sixth period the topic of conversation among her peers moved away from Kelly Spitz and back on to the excitement of the homecoming game on the morrow.

This shift in focus also brought back to Layla's attention her own impending part to play on Saturday night. After sixth period was over, Layla made her way home in silence. This would be, she surmised, the longest weekend of her life.

Layla was sitting in her room casually looking over the clothes hanging in her closet when she heard the phone downstairs ring. She thought nothing of it, for her parents had frequent callers. For the moment, she had some very pressing concerns: what to wear on Saturday.

She didn't want to wear anything fancy. She didn't want her peers to know that side of her. They didn't have the right. At the same time, she would undoubtedly be under some sort of spotlight, however briefly, and she didn't want to add fuel to the fire of ridicule – ridicule that she would undoubtedly be made to feel when Linda or one of the others were crowned the Most Popular, while she would dutifully be made the slink back in that hole of self-despair she had gotten used to.

Layla was awakened from her daydreaming by the sound of her father's voice. "Layla," came the call from down the stairs. "Can you come down here? It's your school. They're on the line."

"Oh great," Layla said ruefully. Then she thought, "What am I in trouble for now?" as she sighed in desperation.

She willed her hand to open the door and walked down the stairs automatically, like a body without purpose. When she reached the living room where the phone was located, she saw her father talking on the phone and her worried-looking mother standing next to him.

Layla stood uneasily at the threshold as her father continued speaking.

"Uh huh. Hmmm. That's really something quite amazing," he was saying to the unknown person at the end of the phone connection.

Layla imagined all sorts of things, but the dominant thought coursing through her nervous mind was that somehow her parents had gotten wind of the whole popularity contest thing. That was the last thing she wanted, and as her father wound down his conversation, Layla noticed her body temperature rising. She was feeling the heat of her own insecurities.

Her father hung up the phone and then asked Layla to come fully into the room. "Layla," he began, "I just heard the most wonderful news."

Layla stood in suspense and had all kinds of excuses forming in her mind for not telling them about the contest and her role in it.

"That was the principal of your school."

"This is it," thought Layla, "I'm cooked now."

Her father smiled broadly at her mother to calm her concern and then looked at Layla and said, "He said you helped save a girl's life today at school. He said you did CPR on her and kept her alive long enough for help to arrive."

Layla shook with unsteady emotion. She had been expecting something else and received something else entirely.

"Allah be praised," her mother cried out and rushed forward to hug her daughter. "I always knew you would do something great someday. I just didn't know it would be so soon in your young life!"

Layla stood there stunned, even as her father came over for his chance to give her a hug. "I, uh…," she stammered.

"The principal said that there'll be a news crew at tomorrow's homecoming game, and they want to interview you," her father added. "I think that's good enough a reason to cancel out on my meeting tomorrow night."

"And I'll leave that party early tomorrow with Hafsa and meet you there at the school," chimed her mother.

Layla was then lovingly forced to recount the whole episode, and while she was in the middle of the story, her brother Ahmad came home and joined the gathering. Layla was sure to leave out any mention of the popularity contest. She also didn't talk about her first meeting about Kelly Spitz and what she knew about her.

When she was finished, her family asked her a lot of questions and congratulated her profusely. Hafsa, who had been napping, awoke and ran into the room asking what was going on. Mercifully, her parents told her that she would find out later and Layla was able to get back to her room on the excuse that she was tired.

Once more in the safety of her inner sanctum, Layla flopped herself back on her bed and tried to make sense of all that has happened. She had never had a month like this one in her life. She was bursting with questions and unable to fathom all that had occurred.

Putting aside all the events involving Kelly Spitz, now her parents were coming to the homecoming game. They would find out everything and see her publicly humiliated, or at the very least they'd see just how unwanted she really was in that school.

She peered hard at the ceiling, trying to follow the paint patterns etched in the plaster. She found herself drifting off to sleep and this time, for once, she didn't fight it. She would sleep soundly for the first time in a long time.

16

"Layla," her father called up the stairs. "Come on, we're going to be late."

Layla was putting the finishing touches on her outfit. She was still emotionally shaken from the events of Friday – and even more stirred up by the events of the three weeks before that! With her blue-jean shirt and loose beige skirt she fancied she was dressing for her own funeral and primed and tweaked her outfit with a morbid sense of humor.

"There," she announced to herself, "that does it." She just finished tying the ends of her *hijab* back behind her head 'pirate-style' and put on her black dress boots before bounding down the stairs. Her father was waiting there by the front door, and to her surprise she saw her brother standing there, as well.

"What are you doing here?" she asked. "I thought you had something you had to do?"

"Don't think that after the great thing you did yesterday that I won't be there to share in your moment of glory," Ahmad said with a wry smile.

"*Great*," Layla thought to herself. "Now my brother will see my defeat."

Layla's father ushered his brood out the door and agreed when Ahmad suggested he drive them in his car. For Layla it was the longest ride of her life. She stared out the window from the back seat and saw the streets and buildings of her town whiz by as if they were the parts of a movie going in fast forward. Layla mused that all of that was like the story of her life: a big blur with hardly any time to catch one's breath.

When they finally arrived at the school, Ahmad found parking a few minutes walk away. "This is where I used to go to school," Ahmad ruminated, to no one in particular. "Wow…everything seems so *small* now."

Layla couldn't quite understand what he meant, but followed along obediently as the trio made its way to the line at the entrance booth. Waiting for what seemed like a half an hour to Layla allowed her time to formulate her strategies for shielding her family from the entire popularity part of the night's events. Perhaps she would feign sickness just before halftime and beg to go home. Maybe she could get her family to go with her to the concession stands when the contest announcements began so she could distract them with food.

Layla was shaken from her plotting by a sudden slap on her back. She turned to find Shamika Thompkins and some of her friends standing there.

"How you doin' girl?" Shamika asked warmly.

"Oh," Layla said curtly. "I'm doing okay. How are you?"

"Who's your friend?" Layla's father asked, turning around to see what was going on.

"Oh, this is Shamika Thompkins. She goes to my school," Layla answered.

"Pleased to meet you," her father said with a smile.

Shamika smiled back and proceeded to talk about how she just met Layla a few weeks before and thought she was a great girl. Layla's father beamed with pride and hugged his daughter as Shamika and her friends scampered off.

After they reached the head of the line and purchased their tickets, Layla's dad arranged with the ticket lady to hold two tickets in reserve for his wife an daughter who would be arriving later. With that done, the trio made their way in to the school's sports field.

Given that it was still late afternoon, well before nighttime, Layla could see the entire field. There was a large grass-covered football field in the middle, flanked by two rows of stands on either side. It looked to her that each side could hold hundreds of people, and the stands were filling up fast.

Everywhere, Layla saw students from her school, and a lot of their parents, too. She had never seen so many people at a school function before, and it only made her feel that much more apprehensive about the half-time program. That was one it hit her, the ticket lady had given a printed program to her father when he bought his tickets.

After they found a space near the lower right end of the right-side bleachers, Layla asker her father if she could see the program. He handed it to her absent-mindedly. He was obviously distracted by all the movement all around him. Ahmad, also, seemed perpetually fascinated with how different his old school haunt seemed to him.

Layla quickly opened the program and scanned it for the half-time activities. While she was looking, she heard the noise of the school band starting its part of the show. Layla ignored them and the sounds of all the spectators around her.

After locating the half-time agenda, she was relieved to see that no actual names of contest participants were there. Satisfied that she might be able to keep her family in the dark about this, she folded up the program and stuffed it in her pocket.

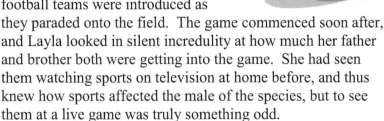

Over the course of the next half an hour, the players of both football teams were introduced as they paraded onto the field. The game commenced soon after, and Layla looked in silent incredulity at how much her father and brother both were getting into the game. She had seen them watching sports on television at home before, and thus knew how sports affected the male of the species, but to see them at a live game was truly something odd.

A little while later, about twenty minutes before half-time, Layla's mother and little sister arrived. After they settled in, Hafsa found that she was happy just yelling along with everyone else, even though she sometimes yelled when there were no dramatic plays to shout for. This made some of the nearby spectators giggle.

All Layla could focus on was half-time, and how there was the strong possibility of her being humiliated - not just in front of the whole school - but in front of her whole family, as well.

She desperately hoped that there were no plans to bring all four girls to the field and talk about each one. She just imagined names being called and hers being booed by the crowd. Her heart started to beat faster, and she felt shaky. She felt like she had to sit down until she realized she was already sitting down. It was then that she made a silent plea to God for strength.

Without realizing it, the first half of the football game had ended, and Layla missed her chance to put one of her schemes into action. There would be no chance for concessions now as the field below them was already filling with cheerleaders and people bringing a makeshift stand and microphone equipment out.

Layla clenched her fists and asked Ahmad if he wanted to go and get something to eat. He indicated that he wasn't hungry, causing Layla to frown. A moment later, a voice came over the sound system. It was Mr. Gottbaum.

"Welcome parents and students of Mansfield Junior High!" he boomed.

The crowd erupted in cheers and it had the effect of elating Mr. Gottbaum in the ways that students were already familiar with.

"And a welcome to Sun City Junior High," he announced, though with less gusto.

The parents and students from Sun City cheered as loud as they could, but due to their fewer numbers it was greatly diminished in intensity. A few of the Mansfield boys in the upper stands booed in jest.

Mr. Gottbaum then proceeded to explain the school popularity contest that had been implemented and its purpose for finding a school spokesperson to preside at fundraisers and other events.

For the first time in her life, Layla hung on every word Mr. Gottbaum said, not that she was so interested in winning, but that she didn't want to hear the dreaded sound of her own name announced as part of his speech.

Despite droning on about the contest for several minutes, causing some people to actually leave the bleachers to head for the concession stands, Mr. Gottbaum never actually mentioned the names of those who were in the contest itself.

Layla felt a tiny bit of relief, and when her mother looked at her and smile, Layla smiled back tentatively. Her feeling of ease, however, was short lived.

At that moment, Mr. Gottbaum triumphantly announced, "And now, without further delay, I will announce the winner of this, our first ever popularity contest."

Layla clenched her fists once more and waited for the inevitable embarrassment that was to come.

"After a heated contest," Mr. Gottbaum went on, "the students ballots have been tallied…"

Layla felt her heart skip a beat in anticipation and dread.

"…and the winner is…"

Layla wanted to close her eyes and run away but her feet seemed glued to the floor.

"Shamika Thompkins!"

Layla stood stunned and mute as the crowds around her erupted in cheers. Shamika came running out onto the field from somewhere, pumping her fist in the air and smiling and cheering for herself.

Mr. Gottbaum called her over to the small portable stage to say a few words, and after a quick victory lap around the stage, Shamika climbed on board and walked up to the microphone.

"Thank you. Thank you. Thank you Mansfield junior high!" she screamed excitedly, much to the delight of the crowds nearby.

Layla came out of her trance and when she realized that she had fully escaped the reality of her worst fears, she looked around, began to smile, and cheered as loudly as her slowly thawing voice would allow. It was then that she noticed her friend Michelle standing near the bottom of the bleachers, alone.

While Shamika continued with her acceptance speech, Layla tapped her mother's arm and pointed to Michelle. Her mother nodded and Layla quickly made her way down the stands to where Michelle was.

When she approached her, Michelle looked at Layla and Layla could tell that she had been crying. Layla gave her a hug and patter her back.

"It's okay," Michelle intoned. "There's always next year." Then Michelle stood up and the look on her face changed completely.

"Oh my gosh," she said excitedly. "I have to start planning early. I can't be seen all depressed and sad." And with that she hugged Layla once more and bounded off, mumbling something about getting her supporters together for pictures.

Layla barely had time to catch her breath when she heard her name. It wasn't said by someone near her, but by a loud mechanical device. Her name was being said over the loudspeakers!

"Come on up here, Deen!"

Layla looked at the field and saw Shamika Thompkins, there behind the microphone, looking straight at her and motioning with her hand for her to go there.

Layla froze for a moment, but then she realized her family was watching her, so she would have to go along with whatever fate was throwing her next.

Her legs moved involuntarily and she willed herself to walk out onto the grassy green football field. She felt a surreal kind of weirdness, seeing the bleachers from this angle, and as she got closer to Shamika, she wondered what cruel tortures she was in store for.

After Layla ascended the stage and was standing next to her, Shamika continued her speech, saying, "And this girl right here. She was the first girl I ever met in my life who told it straight. She said, 'Why are people judging others because of what they look like or dress like?' She told me that being sincere was the true way to know who was good or not. That's real, and this is what the students of Mansfield Junior High are all about."

Then, much to her surprise, Mr. Gottbaum came over from the side of the stage, and with a second mic he added, "And Ms. Deen here, as many of you already have heard, helped to save the life of a student yesterday using what she learned in the CPR classes offered right here in our wonderful school. A local news crew is here right now to cover the game, but also to interview her about how dynamic and exciting our students really are."

Layla stood silently with eyes wide open at what was happening. Then she noticed a television news camera about twenty feet away and wondered how she would ever remain calm or focused while on TV.

Then the unthinkable happened, as far as Layla was concerned.

"And now we'd like to hear from our very own Layla Deen about her heroic episode."

Mr. Gottbaum held his portable microphone up to Layla's mouth, and out of the corner of her eye she saw someone bringing the television news camera closer.

Layla looked at the crowds of people lining both bleachers. She looked in the direction of where her family was sitting and caught a faint view of them waving to her. She swallowed hard, and then she began to speak, drawing upon all her experiences with past speech competitions in weekend school.

"My fellow students, parents and respected guests," she announced.

The silence of the crowd was deafening in her opinion, and she realized that this was the first time most of them had ever heard a student speaking while wearing a head scarf.

"My name is Layla Deen. Some of you know me, though most of you don't. I'm not very outgoing. I don't have many friends, but I do try to treat everyone with respect. I believe that a person should be judged by their actions and not by their outward appearances."

At that remark, a few people clapped in the stands.

"Yes. I helped a girl yesterday who needed it, but I was not the only one there. I just took the lead in opening myself up to what another person needed. We all have to help each other in our times of need. Too often we see people who are hurting or who are in pain, and we pass them by, thinking that it's not our problem. Well, a problem for one is a problem for all, and without each other we all are victims of unsolved problems."

People here and there throughout the stands called out in support, and this emboldened Layla.

"The results of the Popularity Contest are in, and I believe the right person was chosen."

Shamika smiled broadly as a crowd of her supporters in the upper left bleachers clapped and hollered in unison.

"If there is anything I would ask all of us to learn from this experience, it's that all people are connected together in the same human family. We sink or swim together, and whether they are the greatest of us or the least of us, all people deserve to be treated with dignity and respect."

The crowds of people in both bleachers erupted in cheers and clapping – even Mr. Gottbaum was visibly pleased and clapping.

"To conclude," Layla said, as the roar of the crowd faded away, "I believe that the most popular people are those who give the greatest service to their fellow men and women. A very wise man once said, 'God does not look to your appearance or your wealth, but He looks into your heart and actions.' My fellow parents and students, are you ready for God to look into your hearts and actions? Join me in making sure that what He finds is good and pure. Let us build a strong school and an even stronger community of people who help each other, support each other and also respect each other with the respect that one person owes to another. Thank you and go with peace."

Layla was stunned at the effect of her spontaneous words upon both herself and the crowd. The stands shook as the people on both sides of the field stood up and clapped and cheered. The number of camera flash bulbs going off was reminiscent of a starry sky at night and the effect was really overwhelming as far as Layla was concerned.

She was relieved to see her family rushing across the field towards her. Before they got there, however, Shamika embraced her in a big bear hug and said, "You rock!"

There was still the promised interview from the TV crew and a lot of congratulations and well-wishing from the throngs, but Layla instinctively knew that the rest of the night would hold no negative surprises.

As her father helped her down off the stage and into the waiting arms of her mother, one word came to her mind, and when she realized what it was, she said it aloud: *Qadr*. Then she smiled.

Epilogue

Two weeks had passed since the momentous events of the homecoming game. Layla felt more confident about herself and more classmates at school spoke to her than ever before. She no longer felt so much like an outsider. Even more than that, the relief of summer vacation was now only a few weeks away. She would be able to prepare herself for entry into high school with a clear heart and an unburdened mind.

Meanwhile, Kelly Spitz was recovering in the hospital. Layla went to visit her a few days after the game to see how she was doing. Before she left, Kelly revealed that it was she who wrote Layla's name on the contest sign-up sheet. When Layla asked why she did it, Kelly explained that she had gotten mad when Layla had accidentally found her doing drugs in the school bathroom.

Layla forgave her and this caused Kelly to cry tears of joy. She explained that in Layla she had found her first real friend. She also proudly announced that her mother had finally thrown out her abusive boyfriend. Life might get back to normal for her after all.

Shamika went on to be a great spokesperson for the school. Linda Patterson lost some of her popularity and was in effect dethroned. Michelle threw herself into weaving her schemes for future victory in the popularity contest and seemed none the worse for her lose. In short, things were very much back to normal at Mansfield Junior High.

Layla ruminated on the events of the school year while lying in her usual position on her bed. When she told everything that happened to her friend Rayhanna, she said the same word that she had said before, the same word that came to Layla's own mouth at the end of her speech on game night: *Qadr.*

Things happen for a reason, and you can embrace the path that opens up before you and make the best of it, or become mean-spirited and hopeless. That is what God is testing us for. Layla honestly felt, for the first time in her teenaged life, that she had truly learned a lesson.

Her musings were suddenly interrupted, however, by a loud banging on the door. Hafsa flung the door open and came running in dressed in a princess costume. "Look at me! I'm a princess!" she yelled with glee. "And I'm the most popular girl in my class! My friends said so!"

Layla looked incredulously at her rambunctious younger sister as she twirled around and danced for no one in particular. "*Qadr*," Layla thought wryly to herself.

Then she made a silent supplication, saying, "O Allah, make her test easy on her. I know, *insha'llah,* that I'll be there to help." Hafsa just looked at her older sister and smiled.

The End

Other Books for Kids by Yahiya Emerick

Layla Deen and the Case of the Ramadan Rogue
By Yahiya Emerick

Somebody's trying to ruin her Ramadan! Layla Deen and her family were just settling in to break a long days fast when their mother came running from the kitchen and cried, *"Someone stole the food for Iftar!"* Layla knew it was a terrible crime and decided to get to the bottom of this mystery. See what happens! Illustrated. Ages 7-12

Ahmad Deen and the Curse of the Aztec Warrior
By Yahiya Emerick

Where is he? Ahmad Deen and his sister Layla thought they were getting a nice vacation in tropical Mexico. But what they're really going to get is a hair-raising race against time to save their father from becoming the next victim of an ancient, bloody ritual! How can Ahmad save his father and deal with his bratty sister at the same time? To make matters worse, no one seems to want to help them find the mysterious lost city that may hold the key to their father's whereabouts. And then there's that jungle guide with the strangely familiar jacket. Are they brave enough—or crazy enough, to take on the Curse of the Aztec Warrior? Illustrated. Ages 9-14

Ahmad Deen and the Jinn at Shaolin
By Yahiya Emerick

A once in a lifetime chance! Ahmad Deen is one of ten lucky students in his school who gets an all-expense paid trip to China. But instead of *getting* a history lesson, Ahmad may become a victim *of* history as he is thrust in the middle of a bizarre web of superstition, corruption and ancient hatreds that seek to destroy all who interfere. Who kidnapped his room-mate? What clue can only be found in the Shaolin Temple? How will Ahmad learn the Kung-Fu skills he'll need to defeat the powers of darkness. or will he fall prey to the mysterious *Jinn at Shaolin?* Illustrated. Ages 9-14

Isabella: A Girl of Muslim Spain
By Yahiya Emerick

A classic tale about a young girl who finds Islam, and danger, amidst the harrowing religious conflicts of medieval Muslim Spain. Experience firsthand what life was like in the splendid Muslim city of Cordoba. See through the eyes of Isabella as she struggles with her father's beliefs and finds that life is not always as easy as people think. Embark on a journey into history, into the heart, as you follow her path from darkness into light. Illustrated. Ages 10-16

The Seafaring Beggar and Other Tales
By Yahiya Emerick

A delightful collection of short stories, poems, essays and other writings that showcase a variety of themes and inspirational nuggets of wisdom. Many of these stories and poems have been published in international magazines and are sure to put a smile on your face and a warmth in your heart for the beauty that is Islam. Illustrated. Ages 10-14

Muslim Youth Speak: Voices of Today's Muslim Youth
By Yahiya Emerick

What do Muslim youth today think about Islam? What are their suggestions for living and promoting it? What are their observations about the state of Islam in America today and how to make it grow? This book is a compilation of essays, plays, exhortations and other writings by actual Muslim youth. Find out what's going on in the minds of the second generation! For Junior High level.

The Story of Yusuf
By Yahiya Emerick

Finally! The most beautiful story translated for today's English-speakers. Enjoy the sweep of Allah's revelation as you follow the adventures of Prophet Yusuf as he embarks on a harrowing journey that begins with betrayal and ends in a display of ultimate forgiveness. Illustrated. Ages 9-12

Full Circle: Story and Coloring Book
By Yahiya Emerick

What do you do when... Rashid is going to the Masjid for prayer. But on the way he finds an old woman who needs help. If he helps her, he will be late for prayer. If he does not help her, he will miss doing a good deed. Should he help the old woman or should he get to prayer on time? Find out what he does in this wonderful story about going full circle. A strong moral tale showing young children how to continue to do good deeds even when they are worried about keeping other responsibilities. Illustrated. Ages 5-7

In the Path of the Holy Prophet
By Yahiya Emerick

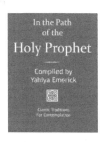

A collection of 57 sayings of the Prophet Muhammad on subjects related to spirituality, meditation, the other world and how to live rightly. Fully illustrated to enhance the impact of the text. For Junior High and High School level.

The Holy Qur'an for School Children: Juz 'Amma
By Yahiya Emerick

A complete textbook for learning and understanding the last section of the Holy Qur'an. Every surah is presented with an engaging introduction, a clear explanatory translation for maximum comprehension, review questions and activities to test the knowledge of the students on the themes of each surah, the full Arabic text and finally, a phonics-based transliteration system is given which is the easiest method for pronouncing the sounds of the Arabic text. Illustrated. Ages 8-16

Color and Learn Salah
By Yahiya Emerick

A complete guide to learning how to do prayers combined in a coloring book format. Covers the complete prayer including ablutions, supplications and movements. Illustrated. Ages 6-8

How to Tell Others About Islam
By Yahiya Emerick

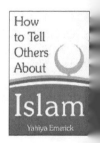

A manual of technique, advice and inspiration on how to communicate Islam to non- Muslims. Topics include how to approach different ethnic groups in North America, how to prepare for giving da'wah, how to handle other religions, as well as many others. Several appendices offer lists of the most effective and readable Islamic literature currently available in English. Illustrated. For High School level.

My First Book About Eman
By Yahiya Emerick

A first grade textbook on Islam that lays a solid groundwork for children in learning their faith and the reasons why it is important. Lessons are friendly, focused and provide excellent starting points for further enrichment and exploration of the faith. Illustrated. Ages 5-6

My First Book About Islam
By Yahiya Emerick

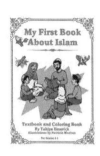

This is the second grade textbook on Islam that builds upon the lessons taught in the first grade textbook. The Islamic worldview is introduced with an emphasis on learning the basics of Islamic religious duties and practices as well as what it means to be a Muslim. Illustrated. Ages 6-7

Learning About Islam
By Yahiya Emerick

This textbook covers all the fundamentals of Islam and is arranged into clearly defined lessons and units. Review exercises at the end of each lesson provide ready-made homework assignments and unit review exercises prepare students for unit tests. A stunningly beautiful book by the same author as the popular textbook for older children, "What Islam is All About." Illustrated. Ages 10-12

What Islam is All About
By Yahiya Emerick

The standard textbook on Islam for grades 7 to Adult in much of the English speaking world. This book covers all the major beliefs, practices and related material that would make one well-versed in the Islamic way of life. These fascinating lessons introduce students to a variety of aspects of Islamic belief and history that makes Islam relevant and fun. Illustrated. Ages 13-Adult

A Journey through the Holy Qur'an
By Yahiya Emerick

A modern free-flowing translation that addresses the needs of the modern-day youth. Easy to read and with helpful background information on the various passages of the holy book. 12-adult.

The Complete Idiot's Guide to Rumi Meditations
By Yahiya Emerick

An exploration into the Islamic dimensions of Rumi's life and thought. This book presents many of Rumi's poems that relate to the Islamic way of life and discusses how to draw faith-lessons from his voluminous work. An excellent book for Junior high school to adult.

Muhammad
By Yahiya Emerick

The story of the Prophet Muhammad told in the form of a narrative. This biography has been acclaimed as the most balanced and easiest to read book of its type on many websites all over the internet! Step back in time as you enter 7th century Arabia and find out why. For High School level to adult.

The Complete Idiot's Guide to Understanding Islam
By Yahiya Emerick

A complete overview of Islam and its worldview in an easy-to-access format and style. Excellent for high school through adult reading levels and also great for *da'wah*. Illustrated.

The Meaning of the Holy Qur'an in Today's English
By Yahiya Emerick

Finally, a modern translation and commentary that fills the needs of the present while paying due respect to the understandings and methodologies of our pious predecessors. This work contains reasons for revelation, voluminous footnotes and commentary as well as a large number of extremely useful resources – all encompassed by a flowing and natural style of modern English. Ages 14-adult.

Made in the USA
San Bernardino, CA
10 November 2012